Stars Still Fall

Jules Kelley

STARS STILL FALL

Copyright © 2023 Jules Kelley

All rights reserved.

Cover art by Tayler Parkin, @artby_tayler on Instagram

Cover design by Jules Kelley

Proofread by A. Thompson, arthompsoncentral.com

This is a work of fiction. Any similarity between the characters and situations within its pages and places or persons, living or dead, is unintentional and coincidental.

https://juleskelleybooks.com

Contents

*This book is dedicated to
all rural, country, redneck, and/or Southern queers,
the ones who couldn't wait to leave and the ones who stayed,
the ones who knew all their lives and the ones who had no idea,
the ones we lost and the ones who are
still breathing—
With all my love, from one of your own*

ONE

Gideon, Alabama
1995

JOHNNY'S DOUBLE-WIDE WAS BUTTED RIGHT UP AGAINST THE back of the junkyard way out on the edge of town, no neighbors for at least half a mile, so whoever was knocking at my door early on a Tuesday morning was there on purpose. Probably to buy a pie.

I was up to my elbows in pie crust, with my hair slipping out of its barrette into my eyes. I looked a mess, but a sigh only blew the flour up in a cloud around me, and my bangs didn't budge at all, so I just yelled, "Come on in! Door's open."

The screen door screeched as it always did when it opened, sounding like a scalded cat. I should probably get Johnny to grease that someday, but it was nice to have a warning that someone was coming in.

"I ain't got the first batch in the oven yet today, but you're welcome to sit and…" I turned to see who had dropped by, and my tongue stuck to the roof of my mouth. I wiped both hands on my apron, automatically hiding the right one behind the smudged fabric. "Aunt Pauline. Didn't expect to see you here."

My mother's sister didn't much care for my decision to live in sin with Johnny Meadows, among other things, and the last time I'd seen her was at the Easter pageant at the Baptist church across town, when she'd moved to the other side of the aisle just so she wouldn't have to sit anywhere near me. *"Heaven knows I tried my best,"* she'd told Mrs. Dawson, the pastor's wife, *"but she's in the Lord's hands now."*

I'd been so humiliated I'd excused myself to the ladies' room before the pageant even started, and I hadn't come back in. Afterward, Johnny told me I'd missed his cousin's six-year-old son dressed as Jesus riding a Shetland pony straight into the church, but all I could think was that my aunt thought I was more *unclean* than the horse shit they'd had to shovel off the carpet.

"Well," Aunt Pauline said now, clutching her bag like she thought I might make a grab for it. Couldn't be too careful with us sinners, I guess. Sure, I was only living with a man I wasn't married to, but I might turn to thieving next if that got too boring. The two fingers I had left on my right hand might end up sticking to her pocketbook and pulling out her cash—only moderately less precious to her than her eternal soul. *Maybe.* "I didn't expect to come out here myself, but you got some mail, and it looked like it might have to do with the estate."

I swallowed hard, clutching at my floury apron. "The estate's been settled for years now," I said, and my voice sounded tinny, like it was ringing in my ears. I willed the noise to stop; it paid me no mind. "Just leave it on the table, then. I'll take a look at it when I get a chance."

She crossed the threshold into the kitchen like she thought she might catch fire just from being in the same room as me, and I tried hard not to roll my eyes. She eased a large white envelope down onto the table, and I held my tongue when I saw her reading the mail that was already sitting there. Johnny had been going over the checkbook last night, so it was probably just bills laying out, but I didn't like her sticking her nose in my finances. Or anything about me, really.

"You want something to drink before you go?" I offered, not because I wanted her to stay and judge me some more, but because she'd judge me more if I *didn't* offer. "I got ice tea in the fridge. Got some peaches, fresh from IGA—"

"No." She cleared her throat and finally let go of the envelope, though she was slow stepping away from the table, and I finally understood why she'd brought the mail over instead of having someone else deliver it, instead of writing my forwarding address on it and sticking it back in the mailbox. She wanted to know what was in it.

Tough luck.

It wasn't that I didn't feel bad for Aunt Pauline. She'd lost her little sister five years ago, after all, but I'd lost my mother—and my father and brother—and I didn't much feel like having to worry about anybody other than myself when I read that letter for the first time. And most of all, I didn't want to deal with her offering advice or opinions on whatever was in there.

"Well, you're welcome to stay." I made my voice as sweet as I could, sweeter than the berries on my stove as I turned back to check on them. "But I've got to get movin' on these pies or I'll never catch up."

She sniffed, but when I expected to hear a snide remark, I just heard the creak of the screen door opening and banging shut behind her, and I let out a sigh of relief right into my flour. I should open that letter and read it before Johnny got home from work, but I really did need to get some pies in the oven. If I didn't have pies baked, then I didn't have pies to sell to my regular customers, and we didn't have extra money this week.

And if that envelope had anything to say about my daddy's life insurance, we might have even less.

The pot of blueberries and peaches started bubbling on the stove, dragging my attention over to the welcome rhythm of stirring, adjusting heat, tasting, adding a little sugar, a little lemon juice, some fresh mint. *I should turn on the radio.* Anything to keep me from being able to hear my own thoughts. The radio was a minefield, though. And with my hands full in the kitchen, I wouldn't be able to change the station if that song came on. It would be the grocery store all over again, pickle juice and broken glass around my feet, unable to hear everyone asking if I was okay over the sound playing through the tinny supermarket speakers. *Maybe the TV.* But the antenna was busted, and Johnny'd been so tired all week I hadn't had the heart to ask him to climb up on the roof to fix it, so we only got two channels right now, and both of them were snowy.

Instead, I talked to my brother, something that always calmed me down. I couldn't remember when I'd started having these one-sided conversations with him; sometime after the panic attack in the hospital when they told me he hadn't survived the accident and sometime before Aunt P caught me doing it and scolded me for "practicing the occult" in her house.

Soothsayers and those who contact the spirits of the dead defile the houses they live in!

So I'd never done it again when she was home. But it was just my brother. Just Cole. I'd always talked to him, and I didn't see why I should stop just because I was alive and he wasn't.

So I told him about the pies I was baking, and some of the recipes I wanted to try. I told him about some of my customers from the past few days, including the ones who wanted a "deluxe" pie—the kind that came with a side of fortune telling. If I was going to hell for practicing the occult anyway, might as well make it worth the while, right?

"Mindy asks the same question every time," I told him. "When's she gonna meet 'The One'? Answer's the same every week, but she keeps asking. Guess she's hoping it'll be different one day. Can't really blame her. I'm too scared to ask if I'll ever get out of Gideon, like we used to talk about—don't know what I'll do if I don't like the answer."

I started laying the latticing across the top of the pie filling, careful to get a perfect basket weave. I still felt a little odd charging people for pies, but if I made them look pretty, I felt better about it. Beth and Donna had been the ones to suggest it to me about a year ago, when I'd fretted about not contributing to expenses. *"You've always liked baking, Lilly Ann. Everybody always used to ask if you were bringing one of your pies to the potlucks. I bet they'd pay for 'em."* Most everybody probably bought them out of charity, but charity money paid the bills same as any, and it gave me something to do with my hands while I talked to Cole.

"I'd worry about leaving, even if the cards said yes, I think. Johnny works real hard to take care of me, just like he promised you. He's been working a lot of extra hours lately, so it's real quiet around here. I don't mind, except when he's gone after dark. There's some odd noises in the junkyard at night. Remember that time we camped out in the backyard and scared ourselves silly, jumpin' at every little noise—"

POP

It had come from the living room. There were no footsteps, no voices calling out. A soft electronic hum, like the television turning on, started up in my ears. Maybe it *was* the TV, and the popping sound had been the screen door closing. Johnny could keep it from squeaking sometimes, and a few of my customers had young children who could creep in, quiet as a mouse when they wanted to be.

"Johnny?" When there wasn't an answer, I wet my lips and took a deep breath. No need to get upset. Just had to finish putting this tray of mini-pies into the oven, then I could go see who it was. "Andrew? Kaylee?" Donna's kids always went straight for the TV and our worn-out copy of *Bambi* whenever they were over. But I didn't hear *Bambi*, and I didn't hear static. I closed the oven door and rounded the corner into the living room.

I don't know what I expected to find, but seeing the room empty was more unnerving than whatever else might have been there. I stood still for a minute, listening, rubbing the smooth knuckles of my right hand against my hip, pressing against the bone where there used to be three fingers, running the soft bumps over my pockets.

The little red indicator light on the TV was on, but the screen was blank. No picture, no sound, no snow. Just black. I pressed the power button, and it flickered and went dead. I pressed it again, and the picture blinked into view, jumpy and staticky, Judge Judy's voice warbling through the warped images. I turned it off again and let out a breath. Probably just a weird power surge. Wouldn't be the first time out here.

I should get back to the kitchen and start working on the next batch of pies, but I cracked the screen door open carefully so it wouldn't screech—*See? It can be done. Nothing to worry about*—and squeezed out onto the porch to get a breath of fresh air. Fresh, *humid* air, with the temperature quickly climbing as the sun burned off the morning fog and really got going for the day. But the last of the honeysuckle was still blooming, and the blackberry bushes down at the end of the house were fruiting. They'd be perfect for pie filling in about two or three days, once the last few red and purple spots deepened into that summer-night shade of ripeness. It might be hot, but it was still gorgeous, rich with fragrant sap and fat cicadas buzzing.

I hadn't gone into town since the third Sunday in April, and the end of August was burning up quick as a handful of pine needles in a bonfire. By mid-afternoon, I was going to want that oven turned off and cooling unless I wanted to be a puddle, which meant I needed to get back inside and get to baking. Sooner today's quota was done, sooner I could turn the damn thing off.

But I took a minute to stare down to the end of the dirt road where it turned off onto a single lane of cracked asphalt. Beyond that was the road into town, which was also the road *out* of town, all the way to Meridian. An acorn pinged off the roof of the old green Chrysler in the driveway, sitting up on cinder blocks so Johnny could work on it in his off-hours. He'd rescued it from the junkyard two years ago and kept saying he was going to fix it up, put a new alternator in it, maybe a new transmission, and it could be my car so I wouldn't be stuck out here by myself. I could drive into town if I wanted to while he was at work.

Just the thought made my heart pound, my palms sweaty.

"Lil's got brown eyes, dontcha?"

My father, smiling at me in the rearview mirror, winking like we shared a secret between us while Mom changed the radio station so she wouldn't have to hear Van Morrison sing.

"Jim, look out!"

I covered my ears like it could block out the memory of screaming metal, shattering glass, and then closed my eyes when that didn't work.

Breathe, Lilly Ann.

I knew it wasn't really Cole's voice. I knew it was just my own thoughts, but it sounded like my brother, and it anchored me like he always had. I focused on it, chased the memory of happier times I'd heard it—pushing me into the pool at the YMCA and then lying to the lifeguard that he'd been trying to keep me from slipping in. Giving me his dessert at dinner because he "didn't have a sweet tooth," when we both knew he had a package of marshmallow Pinwheels stashed under his bed. Promising me that even after he was deployed, he'd write me letters, and that he'd told Johnny Meadows to keep an eye on me, make sure nobody gave me a hard time at school.

That did it. Finally, I was back in my body—scarred and missing a few pieces, but still alive, standing on the front steps of Johnny's trailer. The sound of tires on the asphalt made me flinch but pulled me back even more, reminded me of the pies I had in the oven and the rest of them I had yet to make. The car passed the dirt turnoff, so not one of my customers, but I still needed to get back to the kitchen.

I let the door screech when I opened it this time, and I couldn't help glancing at the television as I passed it. Still dark and quiet, as it should be. I envied it; wished I had a button I could push to make my mind go just as silent. The envelope on the table shone bright, almost golden, in a beam of sunlight from the window, but I'd wasted enough time already. And if Aunt Pauline was right and it *was* about the estate, then I needed to have my work behind me when I opened it, because God knew I wasn't going to be able to do anything afterward, and I didn't need Donna or Mindy—or God forbid, Aunt P coming back—to find me crying under the table.

Pies first. The breakdown could wait.

Two

Customers were slow arriving, so while the second batch of pies—full size ones, this time—was in the oven, I unlocked the drawer on the little side table beside Johnny's teal recliner and got out my deck of cards, peeling the old velvet cloth from around them. They seemed to read better if I warmed them up first, and Mindy would probably be along a bit later, as usual.

The image on the front of the scuffed yellow box was worn thin, but I could still see the man holding up his staff. The cards had been a gift from my piano teacher, Miss Agnes, when I left the hospital after the accident.

I'd taken three years of lessons from her, from age nine to age twelve, and I'd been fascinated by the table of decorations she put out every Halloween: spidery lace doilies, black candles, a book of "spells" that were really just recipes written in beautiful calligraphy, a glass orb on a pedestal covered with a velvet cloth, and a box of cards with pretty pictures on them. The cards had come from Italy, she'd told me, and described the mysterious woman who'd given them to her, a *strega*, a witch skilled in folklore. I'd sat, enraptured, imagining it like a scene from a book or a movie, a bent old woman with a colorful scarf covering her white hair, weathered hands shaking as she gave the box to Miss Agnes and told her they were magical cards, to take them far from Rome and to another country—

"She had a little shop on a side street, overflowing with flowers and herbs and statues of the Virgin Mother, and I bought the cards there because the other girls thought it would be fun to tell each other's fortunes on long flights."

She'd done a lot of traveling as a stewardess for Pan-Am when she was younger, and she always had stories to tell. I'd been more interested in hearing about that than I had been in learning to play anything on the piano, even if they were never quite as fanciful as I'd liked to imagine.

When she moved out of her old house into a smaller apartment the summer after the accident, she'd held a yard sale to thin out her worldly possessions. I stayed home when Aunt Pauline went, and Aunt P had come home empty-handed and full of side-eyed opinions about what kind of woman Miss Agnes was based on the items she'd been selling.

A week later, Miss Agnes brought me the box of cards wrapped in the rich blue velvet that used to cover her crystal ball.

"I remembered how you used to like looking at the pictures," she'd told me. *"Your aunt said you've been real down lately. Understandable, of course. But I wanted you to have these. Maybe they'll bring you luck."*

I didn't have to be told that Aunt Pauline shouldn't know I had them, but alone in her guest room with porcelain angels staring down at me from the top of the antique cherry wardrobe where her winter clothes were nestled in among the mothballs, I read the little book front to back, back to front. And on the days when all I wanted was to crawl inside that wardrobe and wait for the moths to eat *me*, I stared and stared at the picture of the man on the front of the box. The Magician. He looked so much like my brother. I think I'd started drawing cards from the deck to see if Cole would say something to me through them. Anything to feel less alone.

Other than Tuesdays, I mostly pulled them out when my mind felt like a prison. It centered me to mix them up a bit. The tap, tap, tap of their worn edges against my palms, the whisper of the slick surfaces sliding over each other, was as comforting to me as the evening call of a whippoorwill or the smell of sweet cinnamon on a winter morning.

They always seemed to know just what to say, too. It was one of the reasons my "deluxe" pies were popular—at least, with the customers who wouldn't think I was going to burn in hell after my aunt got done burning me at the stake. I still don't know who'd started spreading the word around, but I had two or three regulars who didn't even care what pies I was baking as long as they could sit on the other side of this table and let me read the cards for them.

I meant what I'd told Cole earlier, though; I never asked the cards any questions for myself. Didn't want to know what the answer might be. I was as afraid of hope as I was of despair; either one could crack my heart like an eggshell. And if I knew what the cards had to say, I was afraid it would come true. That the mere knowledge would set me on a path I couldn't step off of. What would I do if they told me I'd never leave Gideon, that I was doomed to live and die in this nowhere town?

What would I do if they *didn't*?

As I shuffled, keeping an eye on the driveway for any customers, my mind wandered to the envelope sitting on my table. I didn't want think about what might be in there, but the idea that we might be losing my father's life insurance payment—

Tap.

I fumbled the deck, and a card slipped out onto the table. The Tower. *Upheaval. Sudden change. Chaos. Revelations.*

My pulse thudded in my ears so loud I almost didn't hear the crunch of gravel under tires, and I scrambled to put the card back into the deck, like I could undo what I'd seen. *No. No.* The deck slipped in my hand, and two more cards fell out.

Six of Cups. Eight of Wands.

Someone is coming back to their hometown. A past love is returning.

A car door slammed outside in the yard. I shoved the cards back into their little box and into the drawer of the side table. My hands shook; the drawer stuck as I tried to shut it. Footsteps on the grass, on the cinderblock steps, on the sagging porch.

"Mornin', Lil," Beth Travers said as she rapped politely on the aluminum frame of the screen door before she opened it to let herself in. The screech of the hinges covered the sound of the table drawer finally slamming closed. "I expect you've heard the news?"

"News?" My voice sounded surprisingly normal for having had to find its way around the heart lodged in my throat. "What news? You're the first person been here all day."

The specter of Aunt Pauline that was never far from my mind frowned in disapproval at that white lie, but since she also disapproved of gossip and hadn't shared any, she didn't get to count as a visitor.

"Miss Agnes Randall passed in her sleep. Weren't a surprise, really. Her daughter Debbie said she's been getting her affairs in order over the past week or so, so she must have been expecting it. Still. Sad state of things."

My hands burned with the echo of the cards and my ears rang with the memory of their soft sound as they fell to the scratched paint. I hadn't thought of Miss Agnes while handling those cards in ages; had her spirit paused near me to say goodbye—or to leave a message? (*The Tower. Six of Cups. Eight of Wands.*)

Beth was still talking, something about funeral plans, which song she thought somebody should sing, but I didn't really hear her until—

"Of course, I guess her great-niece will be the one singing. You'd think they wouldn't let her in the church, but then again, nobody ever could say no to Jo Whitaker."

Oh God. My head swam; my ears rang. My heart beat so fast I had to put my hand over my chest to keep it inside my ribs.

"Oh—oh, Lilly Ann, of course I don't mean—" Beth shook her head, reached out to pat my shoulder stiffly. "You and Johnny been together so long, I'm sure he's forgotten all about her."

We both knew she was lying. Nobody could forget Jolene Whitaker —and Beth had been right the first time: Nobody could say no to her, either. Especially not if they'd been so hot and heavy with her in high school that their classmates had joked about them setting off the fire alarm just by being in the same room together.

Eight of Wands.

Six of Cups.

The Tower.

Just a few minutes ago, I'd been thinking about how much I wanted to find a life beyond the one I had, to rediscover my childhood dreams—to see the world, or at least more than this dustbitten corner of it, maybe find out what I wanted to do or be. But now that I could feel a tremor in the foundations, all I wanted was to keep my little home from collapsing.

* * *

By the time my customers for the day had come and gone and all I had left was one egg custard pie that Johnny would be perfectly happy to eat by himself, I'd heard the news of Miss Agnes's passing and Jolene Whitaker's imminent return a grand total of twelve times. About three of those dozen had managed to be tactful about the fact that my boyfriend's ex-girlfriend was about to be back in Gideon for the first time since she'd broken his heart and left us all behind the day after they graduated high school.

Beth and Tammy had both tried to assure me that Johnny's heart belonged only to me, that having his flame-haired ex-beau show up in town five years after she'd hotwired her daddy's old truck and laughed as she burned rubber on the highway wouldn't make a difference in our lives at all. It was sweet of them, but we all knew none of us believed it. Not me, not Beth or Tammy, and probably not Johnny either. If he even knew yet.

It was enough to make me finally reach for that envelope on my table, my name and Aunt Pauline's address typed very impersonally on a label stuck to the front. The postmark was from Meridian, but then, what *didn't* pass through Meridian? That didn't offer much of a hint. I turned it over, my breath stuck in my throat as I unbent the brass clasp and worked my finger under the tongue. The glue popped open, and I paused, trying to brace myself. This was the last moment before I would know for sure what terrible news awaited me.

But maybe if it was bad enough, I wouldn't have to talk to Johnny about Jo Whitaker coming back to town and the way I was already bargaining with myself over what I could endure. Was it okay if he still had feelings but didn't act on them? What about if he acted on them but nobody knew about it? What if everybody knew about it but he didn't kick me out of the house and make me live with my aunt again, or worse, make me find some other man to live with who might not be as kind? What if—

I finished opening the envelope in a flurry, yanking out the papers inside. Something small and shiny thumped into my lap and I slapped at it one-handed to keep it from tumbling to the floor.

The words on the page swam together, and I had to re-read it several times to understand even bits of it through the spidery handwriting.

Dear Lilly Ann—
—the last piece we worked on before your lessons ended—
—always made me think of you—
—hope it can bring you some comfort to think of Cole—

I went to the next page, still trying desperately to understand.

Lilly Ann Guthrie:
My mother had this letter and sheet music in her effects, addressed to you. I found them while helping her get her affairs in order, as she expects to pass soon. Therefore, I am sending them to you, as it was clear she meant for you to have them. I assume she hesitated to invoke the memory of your family too soon, but now perhaps they will bring comfort.
Sincerely,
Deborah Randall Walker

. . .

Behind that letter was, in fact, a book of sheet music for "The Battle Hymn of the Republic" by Julia Ward Howe, with Miss Agnes's own handwritten notes scattered throughout, and with it came the surprising immersion of childhood memory. I was twelve years old, sitting on Miss Agnes's unpadded piano bench, groaning as she set the metronome on the edge of the piano and told me patiently to try again. I hadn't really been enamored of the song—the tune seemed brash and plodding, and I divided my lesson time between plunking impatiently at the keys and trying to wheedle Miss Agnes into telling me more stories about her travels when she was younger.

"When you've made it through the first stanza, I'll tell you about Madrid," I could hear her saying. *"Try it again. With a lighter touch this time, from the top. 'Mine eyes have seen the glory'."*

But my heart wasn't in it. I was learning it for my mother, who wanted me to play it for my brother to sing at our grandfather's memorial service. We'd dropped my lessons altogether before I finished working my way through it, though, since my mother didn't want to pay for something I clearly wasn't going to put effort into, and Cole had sung it without me. Mom had never let me forget it, either.

I looked down at the small, shiny thing that had fallen out of the envelope, and the heavy silver clip twisted my stomach. It had been what Miss Agnes used to hold music books open on the piano rack, and it had a delicate etching of flowers and curlicues along the top edge. It was polished and shiny, and in its reflection I could see the memory of Miss Agnes's disappointed smile when I still hadn't improved, week after week, and my mother's frustrated sigh when she wrote another check for lessons that I wasn't applying myself to.

I had no idea why Miss Agnes had gifted these things to me, when I knew she had other students who had been more dedicated, more talented, and had gone on to better things. Maybe she'd felt sorry for me, as most people in town had. Her letter said she'd hoped it would bring memories of my family, and it did that, even if they weren't particularly good ones. Maybe it had been as simple as that; she'd always been kindhearted.

I didn't know what I was going to do with this sheet music or the clip. It seemed like it should have gone to someone who was going to use it, since I had never planned to play the piano again even before the accident. To heap salt on the wound, I realized as I tucked everything back into the envelope and bent the clasp closed—I was right back where I had been before I'd opened it. Worse, because now I knew I was going to have to attend Miss Agnes's funeral, which meant a whole new mess of complications.

Just the thought of it—the car ride to the funeral home, the crowd of people sure to be there—made my breath go quick and shallow, and I closed my eyes and clenched my fists hard. I'd make it. I had to. I didn't have any other options.

A car door slammed outside, and I jumped. I hadn't even heard anybody drive up, and it was an odd time to be expecting anyone. Too late for pie customers, too early for Johnny to be home, and it'd be a cold summer in hell before Aunt P visited me twice in one day.

I waited, listening, but nothing else followed. No footsteps. No voice calling out. No shadow stretching across the parched grass. Slowly, I put aside the envelope and stood. The scrape of the chair over the linoleum sounded unnaturally loud, even above the thrum of my pulse in my ears. I was at the door without fully remembering walking across the room to get there, out on the porch without hearing the screech of the hinges.

No one was in the driveway. I peered down the red dirt tracks to the asphalt road beyond, but I couldn't see anyone there either. Had I just imagined it? Had it just been an acorn—or a squirrel—on the roof of the brokedown Chrysler? Maybe it had just carried from the other side of the junkyard, even though it had sounded like it was right up under the porch.

I thought for sure I'd have heard if somebody pulled around behind the trailer, but just to be sure, I stepped down off the little porch and peeked around the corner. Nothing but tall field grass whispering in the breeze, the heavy late-summer seeds ticking against the push handle of the lawn mower that hadn't been started since early spring. Johnny had taken his boss up on an offer for overtime that meant he plain didn't have the hours in the day or the energy left over afterward to cut the grass. And despite the fact that I felt silly admitting it, I was scared of the thing since the day the blade had kicked up a little piece of metal and embedded it in a nearby pine tree, where thick sap still oozed from the wound. It had come within inches of Johnny's knee, and I'd lost enough body parts to metal machines for one lifetime.

Out past the overgrown yard was an overgrown stand of scraggly trees, teeming with tangled underbrush and pricker bushes. Years ago, when Johnny's granddad still owned this little plot of land, Johnny and Cole had spent hours out there together as pirates, cowboys, Vikings, whatever they could dream up. I'd been left behind, of course, except when Cole was in charge of watching me while Mom went to the store. Then I'd been the damsel to be rescued or—more often—kidnapped and "imprisoned" by making me sit still and be quiet.

It had been left wild and unchecked for too long now to get back into that thicket. As far as I knew, Johnny had never tried to clear it out after his granddad passed and he had the trailer moved out here. And what was I going to do, grab a machete and hack away at it myself?

The critters were happy enough to take up residence, though, and at least that was a reassurance that nothing more nefarious had made itself at home. Today there were cardinals calling to each other among the branches of the pines. My dad had always said it sounded like they were saying, "Pretty girl, pretty girl." *"Talkin' to you, Lil,"* he'd always tease. I'd rolled my eyes at the time, but these days the memory could usually make me smile. Except today.

Today, the flit of crimson wings through the pine needles was an omen, and the cheerful song a warning: *Pretty girl.* Prettiest girl in Gideon, maybe in all of Alabama, with her long red hair and her deep green eyes, and she'd be in town soon if she wasn't already.

THREE

THE MORNING OF MISS AGNES'S FUNERAL WAS BRIGHT AND
full of birdsong, but I felt every one of Johnny's footsteps through the
house like they were thudding through my soul. If he knew that Jolene
was back in town, he hadn't mentioned it, and I hadn't had the
stomach to tell him myself. Every time I'd almost brought it up, my
throat had closed and the words had soured on the back of my tongue.
The only thing he'd mentioned had been surprise that I'd asked him to
take me to the service.

"Felt like I ought to, is all," I'd said, and he'd taken me at my word.
That had been two days ago, and today I was regretting my decision. I
sat on the edge of our carefully made bed—I'd spent an extra ten
minutes tightening the corners and smoothing the comforter, nervous
fidgeting more than anything—and stared at my shoes, listening to
Johnny fixing himself breakfast.

"Lilly Ann, you sure you don't want nothin'?" he called down the
hall. "Toast, anything?"

My stomach was twisted too tight to put anything in it, and I just
shook my head even though he couldn't see me.

Step. Step. Step. I could hear him coming and I tried—I really, honestly tried—to lever myself up off the mattress, but my body wouldn't budge.

"Lil," he said from the doorway, and I managed a, "Hm?"

He sighed.

"Listen, I'm sure everybody would understand if you didn't go." His voice was soft and quiet, like it always was. Some days I struggled to remember if he'd been that way before Cole died or if he was just still eggshell-walking around me. I hated it, and hated that I still needed it. "It's… Well, it's a lot to ask of you. I could just go and pay your respects, tell everyone you weren't feeling well."

A car ride to a funeral, where I'd have to sit with people who pitied and judged me by turns, was my own special kind of hell, but I couldn't let him go by himself either. If he was alone when he saw Jolene again—when he heard her sing—

"I have to." This time I did manage to pry myself up off the bed, to pick up my purse and catch the strap over my shoulder. "I'll be fine."

I would be. I might white-knuckle the door handle for the twenty minutes it took to get out to the new church building, and my dress might be soaked through with sweat by the end of the service, but it wouldn't actually *hurt* me. Not like it would hurt if I had to move back in with Aunt Pauline when Johnny dumped me for his ex.

The tape deck in Johnny's silver Sunfire was broken, and the radio only got one station. He switched it off before I was even all the way in the car, then he waited until I had my seatbelt fastened before he turned the key in the ignition. So, so careful that it made me tense and anxious, but I couldn't exactly be mad at him for being cautious. He'd been the one to pick me up from Piggly Wiggly the day I'd had to leave after just two hours of being employed as a cashier, when that song had come on the store radio and undone whatever progress I'd made since the hospital. Aunt P had been out and about, enjoying the freedom of not having me moping around at home, but Johnny had answered his phone when Barbara called him from the manager's office.

He'd taken me to the ice cream shop and then to the park so I didn't have to sit in the car to eat my ice cream bar. I still remembered the way it had tasted salty with the dried tears on my tongue, and how the cold sweetness against the roof of my mouth had anchored me into my body for the first time in days.

Johnny had stood staring out at the pond, hands on his hips, and said, *"Promised Cole I'd look out for you while he was deployed. Figure I can still do that, even if he's a little farther away than Kuwait."* He'd turned and looked at me, serious and pale and quiet. *"I know y'all never got along with your aunt. It ain't much, but I moved a double-wide out to my granddad's old plot of land. You could stay out there with me if you wanted."*

Johnny hadn't really been the wild child—Cole had been the instigator of just about any trouble he got into, or sometimes Jolene—but he'd never shied away from a good time if it came looking for him. Sometimes I wondered if he'd still be this somber if he hadn't rearranged his life so I could fit into it. He'd lost his best friend just a few months after his girlfriend had taken off, so maybe he was just as lonely as I was. Maybe that was why I'd let him kiss me that day in the park, and maybe that was why sometimes he turned to me in bed and put his hand on my body like a question, and why I always let the answer be yes. I didn't mind. He never seemed to demand too much of me, and after all, I was living in his house, eating groceries bought on his paycheck.

Now he stared out the windshield, hands gripping the steering wheel, and I listened to the low hum of the tires on the asphalt and felt every popping pebble like a miniature grenade.

It took a small eternity to get out to the new church building, so new it wasn't even finished yet, a whole portion at the back of it still tarped and scaffolded. I hadn't actually seen the chapel—it hadn't been usable for Easter, the last time I'd ventured out of the house—but Aunt P couldn't decide if she was proud of how nice it was or disgusted with how much money they'd spent on it.

The asphalt parking lot was smooth and pristine black, no time to get worn down yet, and in the August sun, it boiled the air like a custard, wet and thick against my skin. I could feel Johnny's attention, his worry, but it wasn't the same building where we'd had the memorial for my family, weeks after their burials, when I was well enough to attend. That had been at the old white cinderblock church with its rickety, hand-painted sign. This soaring brick-and-glass cathedral didn't hold those ghosts.

It held a new specter entirely.

Not *new*. I knew Jolene, of course. In a town as small as Gideon, it was unavoidable, even for a shy, quiet girl who'd read novels under her desk in class instead of making friends. Especially since Jolene hadn't gone a day without somebody mentioning her name.

Jo Whitaker's in detention for saying the F-word to Ms. Bradford.

I heard she almost got suspended for flashing the football team at practice.

No, I thought it was because she got caught in the boys' bathroom. Story is that she was smoking cigarettes, but you know how she is.

I didn't know if she'd done half the things I heard she'd done, but one of the worst fights my brother had with my parents was when Mom tried to stop him from spending time with Johnny. *"I'm just not sure I want you spending so much time around that Jolene girl, and he hardly goes anywhere without her."*

It had been years since high school. People changed. Some people changed so much we could barely leave our houses when we'd spent years dreaming of traveling the world to see all the places we'd read about. So really, there was nothing to say that Jolene was still the impulsive, headstrong siren she'd been as a teenager. Or that Johnny would still be in love with her.

Still.

"Maybe... Maybe I shouldn't have come," I heard myself saying, my voice distant and strangled, my steps slowing as the doors came closer.

Johnny paused, turned, frowned at me. Opened his mouth.

And then—

"Johnny?"

I've heard the approach of thunder like the rolling chariots of an angry god, and I've heard the way a gunshot hangs in the air when you don't know yet what the bullet has hit—and nothing has ever twisted my breath around my ribs like hearing that smoky voice after almost six years.

Jolene.

Johnny whirled so fast it made my head spin, and I felt the total loss of his attention like an icy wind.

"Jo?"

Did he sound—How did he sound? I couldn't tell over the pulsing thrum in my ears.

"How've you been?" *She* sounded distracted, and I watched her look past him to me. She must have cut her hair at some point; it barely touched her shoulders now, but I remembered it in sunset waves down her back. "And—Lilly, I didn't—I heard about Cole and your parents. I'm so sorry for your loss."

My chest squeezed, but I was glad for the reminder of where we were and why. "Thank you," I managed to say. I thought I sounded pretty normal, all things considered. "I'm sorry for yours."

Her smile was grateful, but more than that—it was the first time since the accident that I felt like someone was seeing *me* and not just the ghost of my trauma. And for a held-breath moment, I saw me too.

"We were just heading in," Johnny said, jolting me. I'd almost forgotten he was there. "See you."

Jolene's parted lips and wide eyes said she'd heard the shortness in his tone as well as I had, but she just said, "...Yeah. See you."

I only stole one glance over my shoulder as Johnny caught my hand and pulled me along toward the doors. Jolene's eyes met mine across the shimmering lot, and I all but felt my body turn to salt, crumbling in the heat.

"Sorry," Johnny muttered as we passed through the glass doors into the foyer, and the industrial-grade air conditioner swept the sweat right off my skin, leaving me nearly gasping from the chill. "We can still leave if you want."

"No, it's..." The doors into the sanctuary were propped open, and someone's preteen was standing there offering us a folded paper program. I took it. "It's fine."

The interior of the sanctuary was just as sprawling as the outside suggested it would be, with plush steps leading up to a wide dais. There was an organ on one side of the stage and a piano on the other, and a carved oak pulpit stood somberly in the center. There was enough room in front of the dais for just about anything, including a casket—which was there now. With a church this big, I guess there was no need to pay a fee to the funeral home for a viewing.

There were three whole columns of pews fanning out across the room, with aisles in between them. Aunt Pauline was front and center, just behind the rows reserved for family, so I headed toward one of the right-side pews toward the back, on the outside corner. I tucked myself against the polished pale oak arm, the rough-woven burgundy fabric of the seat cushion scraping my knuckles as I adjusted my skirt under my thighs.

Johnny settled beside me, jaw tight, elbows braced on his thighs and hands clasped. I had no idea how to read him, and honestly, I didn't even want to try.

"Sorry," he said again after a minute. "Didn't figure I'd ever see her come back to this town."

Death tends to change people's plans, I thought, but my tongue was stuck to the roof of my mouth, so I just nodded.

"Guess I probably sounded rude," he continued, squinting up at the sunny frosted-glass window. "Didn't mean to."

"You were just surprised." My voice felt small and flat in the echoing space, but he heard me.

"Thanks."

It felt like too much trouble to force my voice out of my throat again, so instead of saying *"For what?"* I just nodded and was grateful when he let it stand.

People clumped together, little groups of two or three around the sanctuary, whispering to each other, their voices carrying but not their words. Funerals were a kind of social event, after all. An opportunity to see people and talk about your memories of the deceased, or rumors about them, or your own tragedies if you wanted.

I remembered how angry I'd felt at my family's memorial service, how hard it had been to sit in the front row in my black dress, hands in my lap, and not scream at everyone to shut up, shut *up*—but how it was also the first thing I'd felt since I'd asked the nurse, *"Where's Cole?"* and she'd given me the saddest look I'd ever seen. So I'd held onto that anger, and I'd sat in it and simmered, and for a little while it had felt good not to be numb while I glared at the choir singing "I'll Fly Away."

I wondered if anybody here felt like that. Miss Agnes's daughter, maybe, standing in a corner, talking to the pastor's wife. Maybe Mr. and Mrs. Whitaker, Miss Agnes's nephew and his wife, who were seated in the second row but were turned around to chat to my aunt. Or—maybe Miss Katherine Butler, who had been Miss Agnes's best friend since girlhood, whose husband had died in the same war as Mr. Randall, and whose cakes and cookies had often been used as a bribe in my piano lessons. She sat in the front row, but to the far left, not in a reserved seat with the family. As I watched, she tucked a small, delicate handkerchief under her glasses, dabbing gently at her eyes.

I knew that if anyone here knew how I'd felt, it was her.

I was still watching her when the pastor made his way up the steps to the podium and the hushed murmur of conversation stilled. He cleared his throat and waited until the air was clear of the bump and rustle of people returning to their seats. I bowed my head for the opening prayer, but I didn't close my eyes; I just stared at the crumpled paper program in my hands until the Amen.

Afterward, he lifted his head and announced, "And now, Mrs. Randall's great-niece is here to sing her favorite song, 'The Battle Hymn of the Republic.' Glory, glory, hallelujah!"

Johnny shifted beside me and murmured something under his breath, but my attention was on Jolene as she sat at the piano. The entire sanctuary was dead silent; I heard the creak of the piano bench, the flutter of paper as she moved the hymnal aside, even the soft pads of her fingers touching the keys—and then I was surrounded, lifted, drowning in soft, delicate, haunting notes in a minor key. Surely not the same song I'd struggled to learn; definitely not the sheet music still in an envelope back at home.

And then she opened her mouth and sang.

Battle Hymn of the Republic
Julia Ward Howe

Mine eyes have seen the glory of the coming of the Lord:
He is trampling out the vintage where the grapes of wrath are stored;
He hath loosed the fateful lightning of his terrible swift sword:
His truth is marching on.

I have seen him in the watch-fires of a hundred circling camps;
They have builded him an altar in the evening dews and damps;
I can read his righteous sentence by the dim and flaring lamps.
His day is marching on.

I have read a fiery gospel, writ in burnished rows of steel:
"As ye deal with my contemners, so with you my grace shall deal;
Let the Hero, born of woman, crush the serpent with his heel,
Since God is marching on."

He has sounded forth the trumpet that shall never call retreat;
He is sifting out the hearts of men before his judgment-seat:
Oh! be swift, my soul, to answer him! be jubilant, my feet!
Our God is marching on.

. . .

In the beauty of the lilies Christ was born across the sea,
With a glory in his bosom that transfigures you and me:
As he died to make men holy, let us die to make men free,
While God is marching on.

Four

After the song was the sermon, and after the sermon was the viewing, and after that, the pallbearers took the casket out to the shiny black hearse in the shiny new parking lot for the journey to the cemetery. And through it all, I sat in the corner of the back pew, the cheap copier ink on the program smudging with my sweat.

I knew that Jolene deserved to have the sheet music her great-aunt had bequeathed to me. I knew I was going to give it to her. And I wondered—Johnny's dark hair an inky smudge in the corner of my eye—what else I was going to let her have because she deserved it more than I did.

"Did you want to go to the graveside?" Johnny asked me quietly just before the pastor asked us to bow our heads for the parting prayer. I shook my head but didn't dare answer, able to feel the weight of Aunt Pauline's impending imperious *shush* just at the thought. After the benediction, when everyone began shuffling out of the sanctuary, Johnny headed toward the door but I stopped. After today, I probably wouldn't see Jolene again. I didn't even know where she lived. If I didn't talk to her now, I was going to have to keep that sheet music forever, like a charred ember with a red-hot core of guilt and memories. And I absolutely couldn't do that.

"I—I'll be right there," I lied when Johnny turned to see why I'd stopped. Lied *in church*. The hairs on the back of my neck stood up like they could feel the lightning gathering. "I need to go to the bathroom."

Johnny just nodded. "I'll get the AC running in the car," he said, keys jingling in his hand as he headed for the door. I didn't see Jolene anywhere, and I didn't want to go back into the sanctuary. Too many people. Too many chances to be cornered into an awkward conversation. To see people staring at me. But I couldn't just go out to the car, either, not without being caught in a lie. Desperately, I turned toward the under-construction hallway where the barely functional bathrooms were, the smell of plywood fresh and pungent, the plastic tarps rattling against the sheetrock.

The ladies' room was brimming with a loud, echoing silence, and my shoes tapped sharply against the tile floor, leaving ghostly prints in the thin layer of drywall dust. I braced my hands on the white porcelain sink and stared at the pink insulation between the exposed support beams. I was glad there wasn't a mirror so I didn't have to look into my own eyes. What was I doing?

The sheet music should be hers. It should belong to someone who knows what to do with it. Someone who won't stick it in a drawer because they never want to see it again. Miss Agnes deserves that, at least.

All right, that was true. But I couldn't drive, and I didn't have it with me. What was I going to do, invite her over to the house? The house where I lived with Johnny, who might realize that *he* should also be with someone who knew what to do with him? Someone who excited him, who wasn't afraid to go places with him, who was eager to be with him? Someone who made him feel alive and interesting again, not someone who held him back.

She's probably already gone, I told myself hopefully. *On her way to the graveside. And then back to—wherever she lives now, somewhere better, somewhere things happen.* Like Johnny had said, why would she ever stick around Gideon? She'd hated the town even more than the rest of us, and that was saying something. And she was the only one of us who had made it out. I couldn't imagine that she'd want to stay a minute longer than she had to. After all—

The door banged open, and I whirled to see Jolene standing there, looking just as startled as I felt.

"Sorry about that," she said, fumbling for the handle. "Didn't realize the hinges were so loose."

I swallowed around the heartbeat pounding in my throat and managed a nod. "Guess it's one of the things they haven't finished yet."

We stood there staring at each other until I realized that if I didn't say something, she was going to actually *use* the restroom—why she'd come in, most likely—and then it would be too awkward to say anything at all.

"I have something," I blurted out. Her brow furrowed delicately but she didn't interrupt. "Something that you should have. It's—Your great-aunt left it to me, but you should have it. I don't know... When are you leaving? I can get it to you before then."

A bold promise for someone who didn't drive and who could barely stand to ride in a car.

"Or—or I can mail it to you. Where are you living now?"

"Oh." She actually blushed, fidgeting. Oh God, she probably had come in here to relieve herself, and here I was blocking the only working stall and asking her questions. "I'm—"

"I'm so sorry," I said, talking over her, stepping to the side and gesturing to the open stall. "I didn't mean to hold you up—"

"No, it's okay." She smiled, soft and almost beatific. I didn't remember ever seeing her make that face when we were younger. Maybe Johnny had. "I'm, um, I'm actually going to be in town for a while, though. I'm moving into Aunt Agnes's apartment to finish out her lease. So there's no rush."

My vision tunneled as white noise rushed in my ears, the whoosh of my blood throbbing in my scalp until I could see it pulse at the corners of my eyes. I hadn't realized until just that moment that I'd been hanging onto the idea that if we could get past the funeral, the danger would be over. But she was staying. And now she was staring at me.

"Okay. Um. Well. We're in the phone book. Under Johnny's name."

Her lips parted on a breathless, wordless *Oh*. Guilt crawled through my stomach, claws scrabbling at my gut. "Are you—the two of you, y'all are...together, then?"

It was all I could do not to apologize to her for living with her ex-boyfriend, and an excuse sat heavy on my tongue, but I couldn't make the words form. It felt like she took up the whole room, like even pressed against the sink, I was drowning in the ocean of her presence, struggling to draw a breath. I nodded.

"I see," she said. "All right. I'll—I'll look you up." She inched toward the stall, and I scuttled toward the exit.

The door flung itself open just before I touched the handle, and I jumped back out of the way as Beth Travers almost fell through with a surprised squeak.

"Oh, they need to get that fixed," Beth said, patting down her hair. "Excuse me, Lilly. Didn't mean to run you over."

"It's all right." I sidestepped her, and the stale, warm air of the hallway was a relief on my face. "I—I've gotta go. Johnny's waitin'."

* * *

Tuesday morning, Johnny's yard was so full of cars, it looked like the junkyard had overgrown the fence like a patch of kudzu. I could barely get around the kitchen to make the pies everybody was supposedly there to buy, but they didn't seem to mind—too busy gossiping, standing around in little clumps of excited whispers. I only caught a word here and there, but I knew they were all talking about Jolene.

A storm was gathering outside with dark, heavy clouds pressing down on the sky, and the air was so thick with it I could barely breathe. That, or all the air in the house was being sucked up by a dozen gasbags busybodying about while I labored over my fillings and crusts.

It had started out with just my early morning regulars, Beth and Tammy, then Donna after she'd dropped the kids off at school, and then more people than I knew what to do with.

"I ain't got nothin' out of the oven yet," I'd told them, and they'd all waved me off.

"We'll just catch up while we wait. Don't you pay us no mind, Lilly Ann."

I was one more scandalized giggle away from chasing them all out the door with my rolling pin and making them wait in the yard, rain or no. I was tired of the peace of my house being trampled while they all waited to see if Jolene was going to march herself out to Johnny's trailer in a tight T-shirt with *Homewrecker* scrawled across her chest. At least, that's what it sounded like they were talking about, when I could make it out.

When Beth came into the kitchen to get herself a glass of water, I kept rolling out my crust—no fancy latticework today; I wanted these pies done as quickly as possible—and said, "You told them, didn't you? You heard me and her talking at the funeral. In the bathroom."

"Told them what, Lilly Ann?" But she couldn't meet my eyes when I turned to look at her. "Maybe you just make really good pies."

I don't know what I was going to say, anger bubbling up in my chest, my rolling pin gripped so hard I could feel the splinters pressing into my palms, because at that moment, a car door slammed out in the yard and silence rippled through the house on the heels of a shocked murmur. It got quiet enough I could hear the way the wind was picking up outside.

"Is it her?" someone asked, and despite myself, I felt a chill run over my skin.

"Aw, it's just Mindy," Allison said from her spot near the door, and everyone let out a disappointed noise as the chatter slowly picked up again. Instead of the loud buzz of too many voices to make out, I could hear snips of conversations now, and I almost wished for the overwhelming cacophony back.

"Don't know what I woulda done if it'd been her," someone giggled. I tried to place the voice and failed. "Pushed Maggie Jean in front of me, maybe."

"Don't flatter yourself, Tina," Maggie Jean laughed, and even just the sound of her voice grated over my nerves. We'd gone to school together, and ever since the summer she'd started badmouthing Cole because he hadn't wanted to go to the homecoming dance with her, I couldn't stand to be in the same room as her. It irked me that she was in my house and I didn't even remember seeing her come in.

"I still don't know if I believe it," someone else chimed in. "I mean, we all knew what she got up to in high school."

"Maybe that's what turned her." Tina sounded alarmingly sincere. "Maybe she did it so much she got tired of it and had to try something new."

I had absolutely no idea what they were talking about, but I knew I was tired to death of hearing about it. "I swear to you, Cole," I muttered under my breath as I leaned over the counter. "I'm 'bout to roll them out thinner than this crust."

The pie dough ripped, clinging to the wooden roller, and I stopped dead, eyes closed, and counted to ten to keep from screaming.

"Lilly Ann?" Donna asked, coming closer. "Honey, are you okay?"

God knew what they'd say about me if I had another breakdown. I'd had enough for one lifetime. I still couldn't step foot in Piggly Wiggly.

Eleven...twelve...thirteen...

Not for the first time, I wondered what I'd done to piss God off enough that he let me survive that car crash. Seemed unfair that I was the one still here, having to hold myself together. Couldn't I have just gone with Cole?

Fourteen, fifteen, sixteen—

The trailer shook so hard it felt like it was coming apart at the seams; a bright light seared through my eyelids as shrieks of surprise rose around me, and for a second I thought maybe it had happened, maybe God had finally sent that bolt of lightning after me—

But the gasp and murmur of everyone in my house told me I was still on earth, still very much alive, even if the house was twice as dark when I opened my eyes again. The power was out, and from the follow-up thunderclap, it wasn't coming back anytime soon. I stared at the pot of berries on the stove as the bubbling slowed, and relief spread through my limbs.

The electricity was out. It wasn't coming back anytime soon. Thank God.

"Lilly Ann?" Donna said, her fingers soft and concerned on my arm.

I turned around, dusting my hands on my apron, not even bothering to hide my right hand from anyone's pitying eyes. "Ladies, I'm so sorry, but I don't think these pies are gettin' baked today. I'll have 'em tomorrow for anyone that wants one."

"We ought to go before it really opens up and we all get soaked," Beth agreed, setting her water glass down on the counter by the sink. It was going to take more than that for me to forgive her, but it was a start.

"But I just got here!" Mindy protested.

"Nobody wants to be out in this weather." Bless Donna.

A murmur of general agreement ran through them—I wondered if it was the realization that Jolene wouldn't possibly travel in this storm that swayed them more than their own safety—as they all started shuffling toward the door. I stayed where I was, braced against the counter, listening as they left. A good hostess would see them out, stand on the top step and bid them safe travels, but I wasn't a good hostess.

I listened to them leave one by one, their car doors shutting, the engines starting, the tires retreating down the red dirt driveway to the gravel beyond it.

The following silence was lost in the storm, but I didn't mind. I turned the oven and the stove off, just in case the power did come back on, and set to work getting everything tidied up.

A clatter at the front of the trailer caught my ear, then a ghoulish shriek and a frantic slapping sound. Someone hadn't latched the screen door properly, and it was caught in the wind—my penance for not seeing everyone off. I took off my apron and slung it over the back of a kitchen chair on my way. It was probably Tina's doing. She'd never had any sense.

The door was splayed helplessly open against the side of the trailer, far enough that I couldn't reach it from the steps. The grass squelched under my bare feet, and I moved quicker. It took me a good second to get the fingers of my left hand around the rough metal edge of the aluminum, and the wind fought me for every inch as I pulled it with me. The progress I made was too precious to lose by turning around when I heard the truck pull up in the yard—probably one of the ladies had left their purse and was coming back for it. A good hit from my shoulder, and the damn door finally latched.

The truck door creaked when it opened and shuddered when it slammed, and I stared at the side of Johnny's trailer for a long, long minute while I caught my breath instead of turning to see who it was. God help me if it was Maggie Jean; I'd just as soon let her get blown away. Compared to how hard it was to pull myself together, shutting the screen door had been a sweet summer breeze.

"Lilly?"

Even across the yard, through air so thick it swallowed the sound and through the sudden rush of rain as the skies opened up above us, that voice caught me, tugged and pulled me, turned me around and dragged my gaze to her. Standing beside the same beat-up old truck she'd hotwired all those years ago, the wind sweeping her hair across her face, wet strands of it clinging to the curve of her perfectly bowed lips, she stared back at me.

I couldn't move, even as I felt my clothes growing heavier with the rain soaking in, my hair plastered against my neck, rivers running down my skin. The water on my tongue tasted fresh and sweet, but I could barely swallow it. When she reached for the handle of the truck's door, I finally realized what it must seem like to her—me standing here without speaking, refusing to invite her in—and my breath unstuck from my throat with a gasp.

"Jolene! Oh my God, come in!"

I yanked the door open, the slippery metal nearly escaping my grasp again, and ran inside, chased by the splash of her footsteps in the rapidly growing puddle that used to be my front yard. She latched the screen behind herself as she stumbled into the living room, and I closed the inside door, leaning against it, panting as if I'd been the one to dash across the lawn instead of just up the steps.

Rainwater pooled around our feet, dripping from our chins and noses, and as Jolene pushed her hair out of her face, something broke loose behind my breastbone and soared up into my throat on feathered wings. Before I even knew it was happening, I started to laugh.

FIVE

Jolene stared at me like a startled rabbit, but I
couldn't stop once I'd started; my ribs ached and it was all I could do to
squeeze in a desperate gasp between peals of giggles. Just when I
thought I was winding down, I snorted, and this time she laughed with
me. I hadn't felt anything like this in months, maybe years, maybe ever,
and I was dizzy with it.

She seemed to glow like a candle, and I reached for her, mothlike.
Even soaked through, her arm under my right hand was a shock of
warmth, and my fingers twitched against her skin before I snatched
them back.

The laughter stopped; we both looked away.

I shrank against the door, my arms wrapped around my soggy
middle, cold water dripping off the ends of my hair, and curled my
fingers into my wet dress. My own skin was icy where hers had been a
crackling fire. Had she noticed that I'd touched her with my scarred
hand? *Oh God.*

"I'm so sorry." The apology was a wide enough blanket to cover a
multitude of sins, all of which I'd committed in the five minutes since
she'd driven up into the front yard.

"No, no, I'm sorry for not calling first," she said, delicately tugging her soaked shirt away from her stomach. It clung to her chest instead, and my gaze fixed on the line of her bra through the wet fabric. It was purple.

A flash of memory: girls' locker room my sophomore year, coming back to grab something out of my locker while the senior girls were getting ready for gym class, seeing a messy red ponytail swept across milk-pearl shoulders, satiny purple straps catching a few stray strands...

"I'm still working out some things with the phone company at Aunt Agnes's place, so..." She let go of her shirt, and it slapped against her skin, jolting me out of my stupor.

"Oh! I'm so—Hang on, I'll get some towels."

The hall carpet clung to my wet feet, and the bathroom linoleum nearly slid out from under them. I stopped halfway into the room— Johnny's towel was crumpled on the floor beside the hamper, where it had been for two days. I scooped the tattered old thing up and stuffed it into the laundry basket, hands shaking.

I found two clean towels in the laundry closet and clutched the faded one to my chest. The other I held away from myself in my left hand, a pristine emerald-green offering for the siren dripping in my living room.

"I probably should have waited for a better day," Jolene said as she patted her face dry, down over the constellations of tiny freckles on her arms before she clutched it to her chest, almost hiding. *From what?* "I knew it looked like rain, but Beth Travers told me that you usually sell pies on Tuesdays, so I thought it would be better to come when you were expecting people..."

"Oh," I said, eloquently. So *that's* why everyone had been in my kitchen this morning, and why Beth had looked so guilty. I'd accused her of spying on us in the bathroom, but she'd actually set me up, telling Jolene when to come out and then rounding everyone else up to watch the fireworks. Thunder rumbled through the trailer again, shaking the walls, and Jolene looked toward the window.

"I can... I can go, though," she offered, and I shook my head. The red clay driveway turned slick and treacherous when it was wet, and the wind was blowing hard enough it was likely to snap a few tree branches.

"Might as well wait it out." I scrubbed at my face longer than necessary, the tattered towel a halfhearted shield. On a normal day, Johnny's trailer was fine. It was familiar and comfortable if not luxurious. But now I saw it as I imagined Jolene must: worn and faded, warped and washed out. "Do you…want to sit down? I can bring you a glass of tea, or—"

"Don't put yourself out," Jolene said immediately, the expected answer. A polite dance we'd both watched the adults in our lives play out time and again as we were growing up. It felt a little like playing dress-up to be doing it now.

"It's no trouble, really," was the next step, and I took it. The next move was Jolene's; either *Well, if you insist,* or *No, really, it's okay.*

But she didn't say either one, and her silence snatched my attention away from my home's shortcomings. She had paused by Johnny's teal recliner, one fingertip brushing gently over the threadbare arm of it, lingering over a cigarette burn that had been there long before I'd moved in. Johnny didn't smoke anymore, not since high school. He said it was because it was too expensive, but I had a feeling his grandfather's long decline from lung cancer had played a part as well.

"Sorry," Jolene said when she saw me watching. "I…" She blushed, snatched her hand back with a wry smile. "Memories. You don't realize how much you have boxed away in the back of your mind until it all comes rushing in, sometimes."

"It's all right," I said around the lump of nausea in my throat, my left hand wrapped tightly around my right one. My mind was full of all the things she could be remembering about how that burn was made, about who had made it, and when, and doing what *with whom*—"Are you back for good?"

She winced; an apology leaped to my tongue.

"I didn't mean—"

"No, it's not…" Her laugh wasn't at all the confident, swaggering girl I remembered from high school. It was small, maybe ashamed. "It's just…I'm not sure. My roommate…" She took a deep breath. "My roommate moved in with someone else suddenly, and I couldn't make the rent on my own, so I had to break the lease and—Well, I don't know how long I'll be in Gideon." She stared at her hands, rubbing across the edge of her thumbnail. "I don't know where to go."

I didn't understand the eager surge in my stomach, the way those words felt like hearing a prison door creak open. Maybe it was only to throw another inmate into the cell with me, but the air around me crackled when just a moment before it had been stifling. Was it only that misery loved company? Jolene had always been a legend—she'd gotten out of backwater Alabama, gone somewhere else, made something of herself. What, I didn't know, but it must have been something. And now Gideon had pulled her back in, same as the rest of us. She was no better, no different than me, stuck in the quagmire. More than that—we were both outsiders in the town we couldn't escape. My very bones felt as if they were coming alive, ghosts stirring in the marrow.

"I'm sorry about your roommate," I said, when I could pry my tongue off the roof of my mouth.

"Worse things have happened to better people." She said it so quickly that I knew it was another of those well-known dances, so deeply ingrained it was instinct by now. It was as flimsy a shield as my towel had been, but I wouldn't be the one to take it from her.

I was finally dried out enough that I wouldn't ruin the paper, so I brought the envelope with the sheet music and silver clip to Jolene. I had kept the two letters for myself. "Your Aunt Debbie mailed this to me," I explained as I handed it over. "But I haven't played in years, and I wasn't very good when I did. I'd have no idea how anymore, even if I could."

Jolene glanced at my right hand when I said it, but I didn't read disgust or pity in her eyes. Just understanding of something I barely understood myself.

"I remember when you were learning this," she said. I'd had no idea she even knew I was alive at that point. "Cole kept complaining that your mom wanted the two of you to perform at—a baptism?"

"Funeral," I corrected. "Our grandfather's."

"Right." She smiled fondly as she took the pages out of the envelope. "He kept telling Johnny that he didn't really want to sing it, but nowhere near as much as you didn't want to play it. I thought of y'all, actually, when Dad said Aunt Agnes wanted me to play it at her memorial."

"I never liked the way it sounded," I confessed, sinking down into the recliner as she sat on the sofa. "Until I heard you sing it. I've never heard it sound like that before."

"Thank you." She smiled down at the music in her lap. "Not everyone approved of the arrangement. Or maybe it's that they didn't approve of me." She looked up at me, took in what must have been wide eyes and a fishlike gape, and said, "It's one reason why I wanted to come out when you'd have company. So it wouldn't reflect badly on you."

My pulse thumped doubletime and I could feel my face heating. It didn't seem polite to address the situation head on, to admit that I was worried she would take Johnny back and leave me with nowhere to go. It felt...*disrespectful* to validate the rumors, the speculation, especially right to her face.

She must have taken my silence as the guilt it was, because she added, "In fact, I can go now. You've already been so kind. No one knows I was here, and the rain is starting to let up..."

The rain was nowhere near letting up, actually, and the ditches on either side of the long driveway were steep and unreliable. And I might have wished Jolene hadn't come back and upset the delicate balance of my survival, but it didn't mean I wished ill on her.

"Don't be silly," I said, trying to sound more sure than I felt. More welcoming. Less grasping and greedy and selfishly scared. "Johnny's not even home right now."

"...That would probably just make things worse, if people talked," Jolene said, her voice lilting slower like she was waiting for me to catch up.

"What...? What do you mean?" I asked, my mouth dry. I remembered all the eager, nervous gossip in my kitchen that morning; what did they know about Jolene that I didn't? Was she wanted for murder? Was that the real reason she was back in Gideon, why her roommate had moved out suddenly? Was she going to get me out of the way to get to Johnny?

"You know," she said slowly, her eyes intense now. I got the feeling she wanted me to say I understood so that she didn't have to say it aloud, but I had no idea what she could possibly be talking about.

"No idea what I woulda done. Pushed Maggie Jean in front of me, maybe."

"Don't flatter yourself, Tina."

Did she eat the people she killed or something? This was ridiculous.

"Is… Is all the talk not just because you and Johnny dated in high school?" I asked, feeling small and stupid to have to do so. *Dated* was such a mild word for what they'd been.

"I thought you knew," Jolene said, shrinking into herself, the envelope crinkling in her hands as she tightened her grip. "I thought…" She shook her head slowly, her whole body tensed as if she might need to run out the door the moment she said it. "My roommate wasn't just a friend. We were…involved. Romantically." She paused. "Physically."

Well, that cast her distress about the situation in sharper relief; an unpleasant surprise like she had described would be bitter enough if it had just been a friend. That it had been a boyfriend made it worse. And maybe most people in town thought this made her a Jezebel, but here I was, also not married to the man I was living with. I wasn't going to judge.

"Oh," I said, still unsure why this made it dangerous for her to be here alone. "I'm sorry he—"

"She," Jolene interrupted desperately.

My thoughts ground to a halt, struggling to comprehend, circling in wordless confusion. I had a thousand questions, all stumbling over each other, too many to even finish putting one together enough to ask. My mouth opened soundlessly then closed again, and after a long moment, Jolene gave up waiting for me to say anything.

"I'm a lesbian."

Six

I was already sitting, but suddenly I needed to sit down *more*. I barely knew what the word meant—if she hadn't just told me, I'm not sure I would've been able to dredge up a definition beyond the sharp spike of panic that twisted in my chest, like I was going to get in trouble just for hearing it spoken aloud.

A jolt of lightning lit up the room, casting wild shadows, and I felt the following thunder down in the marrow of my bones. Another clipped right on its heels, this one brighter and louder, something that sounded like an explosion ripping through the air. I looked through the kitchen to the wide back window, expecting to see smoke or flames, but there was just the thicket of overgrown trees bending in the wind, their leaves ripping away one by one. I gripped the arms of the recliner, but my pinky finger scraped across the cigarette burn I'd seen Jolene touching earlier, and I jerked my hand away like it was still smoldering.

"I'm sorry," Jolene said quietly now. "I thought... Well, my mother, at the funeral... Maggie Jean overheard her, and..."

"And now everyone knows," I said softly. "Maggie Jean's always been like that."

"So I thought you knew." Jolene tried on a shaky smile. "Sorry I sprang it on you."

"You don't have to apologize to me," I said immediately. I didn't know which way was up right now, but I knew Jolene didn't owe me anything, much less an apology. "But—you and Johnny, I thought…"

She actually *blushed*, rosy splotches on her flawless ivory skin. "I don't know." She shook her head again. "Maybe it was real at the time, or maybe that's why it was never enough. Sometimes I think maybe I was trying to cover up who I really was, from myself as much as anybody else. Even before I knew. I didn't actually—" She seemed to realize she was crinkling the envelope and spent a moment smoothing it out. It didn't help. "I didn't actually know that I felt that way until —" She cut herself off so sharply I could feel the empty space where a word would be as clearly as I felt my missing fingers sometimes. When she spoke again, I knew it wasn't what she'd been going to say. "Until right before I left. About a month before we graduated, I figured it out."

I had about a million questions, and none of them were appropriate to ask. I guess that's why what came out surprised me entirely. "Where did you go? When you left. I always wondered."

It hadn't been the question she'd been expecting me to ask either, judging by her wide green eyes, a little wet at the corners like she'd been about to cry.

"Oh—um, just Meridian at first," she admitted with a shy little laugh. "But I met Crystal—that's my…roommate—and she was so… I was so…" She blushed again, but different this time, a softer bloom across her cheekbones. It was mesmerizing. "I followed her home to Memphis. I don't think I could have done anything else."

I felt that old familiar cavern yawn open inside of me—something that hadn't been there for years. *Want.* I wanted to see something new. I wanted to know what it was like to slip free and fly, go somewhere nobody knew my name, where every corner hid something unknown, like turning the pages in a book I'd never read before. Living in Gideon was like having just one book to read, over and over, forever. Nothing changed. The ending was always the same. Each chapter, page, and paragraph followed its predestined course every time. Just the names changed, and then only sometimes.

Once upon a time, I would've given anything to leap into a new story. I hadn't remembered being that girl in a very long time, the one who wasn't scared of surprises but dreamed of them. For the first time in years, I saw her again. I almost felt like her.

Jolene was watching me, probably waiting to see if I was going to throw her out into the storm after all—and honestly, part of me figured I should. What if somebody drove by and saw her truck parked in my front yard? What if they told Aunt Pauline?

Well, my dad used to say that what he did was his business, and what other people thought about it was between them and God and the fencepost. And anyway, Jolene had done me a kindness. She'd reached through all of the gossip about how that Guthrie girl had gone a little crazy and found me instead. She'd considered my comfort and my reputation in choosing when to honor my request to come relieve me of a keepsake I didn't want to be responsible for.

The absolute least I could do was to pay her back in kind.

"With the power out, I don't have anything on my plate for a while," I said, swallowing the lingering anxiety on the back of my tongue. Was I more anxious that she'd want to stay, or that she wouldn't? "We could sit and catch up. If you want."

Her wary expression was slow to fade, but when it did, the tiny curve of her smile made me wonder if anybody in high school had ever actually known her, or if they'd just run their mouths about nothing at all.

"You wouldn't mind?" Her voice was so soft I could barely hear it over the rain, but I understood the hopeful look in her eyes just fine. Seems I wasn't the only one desperate for company on the same side of the bars as me.

The conversation was awkward at first, halting, until she figured out that I was content to just sit and listen, and that I wasn't going to be weird about her ex-roommate. If living with someone out of wedlock was a sin, then I was just as guilty as her. Didn't seem to me like it should matter much who the other person was, and I said as much. After that, the floodgates opened, and she only stuttered once over a nervous *she.*

And then somewhere around Graceland, the skies cleared. I'd mostly just let her talk about whatever was on her mind, but my mother loved Elvis and had always talked about visiting Graceland after it opened to the public when I was a kid. Unfortunately, Cole had broken his arm at the city pool the summer we had planned to go, and the hospital bills ate up the money she'd set aside for the trip. We never did make it there, so I asked Jolene if she'd been.

"No, not really. I've driven past it a few times. There were a bunch of tacky Elvis souvenir shops across the street for a while, but I think I heard they're putting in a museum or something now."

I could just imagine what it would've been like if we'd gone—Dad would have made fun of the tacky souvenirs and Mom would've hushed him and treated them like sacred relics. I was young enough I would've probably enjoyed myself, and Cole would've been goofing off and talking in a fake Elvis voice the whole time, especially if he'd managed to talk our parents into letting him bring a friend.

But that had been the summer Johnny had started dating Jolene, hadn't it? The reason Cole had broken his arm had been because he'd been showing off on the diving board, trying to win some of Johnny's attention back.

I only realized I was staring off into space when Jolene cleared her throat and said, "Anyway, it looks like the rain's letting up, so I can get out of your hair."

"Oh." I looked out the window in surprise. Gusts of wind were still knocking stray raindrops around, but the clouds had broken and blue sky was peeking through. It would probably be safe enough to drive. "I'm sure you've got other things to do today than sit around out here. But it was nice to chat. I don't…"

I cut myself off before I had to figure out how to finish that sentence. I didn't what? Have many friends? Get to hear about things other than reheated Sunday gossip? Both were true but sounded entirely too pathetic to say aloud.

"It was nice for me too," Jolene agreed quietly. Probably nice not to be constantly defending herself against half-baked opinions. "Since I'll be in town for a while, maybe we'll get to do it again."

An unexpected surge of anticipation brightened my gloomy introspection. I'd never been very good at making friends; too shy to be the first to reach out, too prickly and wary to keep up my end of an acquaintance. For most of my life, Cole had filled that gap for me, gregarious enough for both of us. Since he'd gone, Johnny had been the only one willing to try, and he did his best, but he was too much like me. I guess it shouldn't have been a surprise that we both found Jolene's company pleasant in some way.

"I'd like that," I said honestly, trailing her to the door as she gathered herself to leave. I held it open for her as she navigated her way down the cinderblock steps, and I watched her pick her way across the soggy yard toward her truck. I waited until she started the engine, then waved as she closed the door and put it in reverse. The words tried to stick in my chest, and my voice was as rough as the gravel road she was headed toward, but I murmured, "Drive safe," to her taillights before I closed and locked the door.

* * *

My legs were coltish and unsteady after she was gone. All I could figure was that it was the leftover adrenaline from the morning I'd had —everyone piling into my kitchen, the storm, the power going out, Jolene bringing up memories of my family.

I had to brace myself on the kitchen counter to stay upright, just staring at the mess I hadn't cleaned up when the power went out. The ingredients *might* be okay after sitting out, but I wouldn't bet anything important on it. Still, I was loath to throw any of it away. I already didn't charge much more for pies than it cost me to make them. If I had to start all over, it was going to put me in a real pinch.

At least the storm had cracked the heat a bit; it wasn't too unpleasant to gather my scattered baking implements as slowly and carefully as I was gathering my thoughts. Alone now, with no one to witness a stray blush or ask what I was thinking of, I could consider everything that had just happened, all I'd just learned.

Jolene had left Johnny behind in Gideon and fallen in love with a... With someone else. It was still impossible to imagine. It was like learning that you could drink a song or wear a river, to learn that a woman could love another woman. I stood still, mixing bowl clutched in my hands, trying to picture what it would be like—

"Lilly?"

The bowl clattered to the counter; my heart punched through my chest.

"Don't sneak up on me like that!" I pressed the knuckles of my right hand to my breastbone as I turned, left hand lashing out with the kitchen towel to punish Johnny for scaring me silly.

The towel snapped against empty air. There was no one there.

"Johnny?" The voice had been right behind me—how had he gotten out of the kitchen so fast? And without me hearing him?

But the living room was quiet. The door was closed, the rug in front of it still askew and damp from my and Jolene's desperate dash out of the storm. No one else had crossed it.

Maybe he was in the bathroom?

No. It was dark, as was the bedroom, and now the silence—usually so welcome, so safe—crept up my spine and sat on my shoulders, coiled tight, ready to pounce.

I waited, but there was nothing else. No footsteps, no voice, no doors opening or car noises outside. Clearly I'd imagined it. *Guilty conscience,* Aunt Pauline would've said.

When I returned, the kitchen was exactly how I'd left it, but it seemed like an alien landscape in someone else's life, winding paths trailing through the chaos leading nowhere.

SEVEN

As far as I knew, Jolene's visit stayed a secret. Johnny
didn't bring it up, and when the next Tuesday came and went without
incident, the would-be pie customers didn't dare broach the subject
either, and the crowd lost interest and left behind just my handful of
regulars. Fine enough; if I never had to see Maggie Jean in my house
again, I could die happy—or close to it. She hadn't even bought a pie.

Despite the fact that Jolene had moved in right across town, my life
went back to normal. I didn't hear any more voices or see any strange,
fleeting shadows where they shouldn't have been; I'd just been worked
up over nothing, it seemed.

But then on Saturday, Johnny decided to fix the TV.

I was folding laundry when he leaned in the front door and called,
"Hey, Lil, come stand at the door and yell up when the picture gets
clear."

I paused, a towel half-folded on my knees. "Yell up where?"

"The roof. I'm gonna climb up and fix the antenna."

Well, it was Johnny's first full day off in a while, and I guessed he
wanted to watch something. I set the basket aside and came to the
front door, standing on the top cinderblock step and staring back inside
at the snowy-screened television. I remembered a week before, that

strange power surge, and felt a chill walk up my spine in the August heat.

The antenna creaked as Johnny twisted it; the snow on the screen wavered and faded and thickened again as I called up periodic status reports—*"Better." "Worse." "Same."*

"Goddamn," Johnny huffed after several fiddly minutes yielded lukewarm results, boots scuffing on the roof, and then the most godawful metal screech tore right through me. My body flushed hot and then cold, my scalp prickled, and my joints ached with the need to *run*.

"Lilly Ann? I said how's it look now?"

I blinked rapidly, focusing on the television screen. It was mostly clear. "Better," I croaked, then cleared my throat. "A lot better. Maybe just a little more in that direction?"

The scraping noise was softer this time as he turned the pole with more caution, but I still shuddered, shaking out the misplaced adrenaline from my hands. Finally, the feed looked as clear as I'd ever seen it look on that old television, and I shouted up to him.

"That's good!"

I breathed out a sigh of relief as I heard him coming back down the ladder and went back to the laundry that needed folding. I was almost done with this load, at least. After that, I didn't know what I was going to do. Maybe I'd re-read a book. I wished the library wasn't on the other side of town, or I might have been able to walk there. For a second, I wondered if I could drive myself there, but I remembered how even the antenna turning too loudly had nearly sent me running for cover and figured that wouldn't go so well behind the wheel of a car.

"Need anything from the store?"

Johnny's voice snapped me out of my thoughts and for the second time in a few short minutes I just stared at him with laundry laid across my lap. "We just went grocery shopping."

Johnny shrugged, but he wasn't meeting my eyes, ruffling his sweaty hair and fanning himself with his shirt. "Some of the guys are gonna come over and watch the game this afternoon. Gonna pick up a six-pack and maybe some chips and dip."

I hated the way I automatically calculated how much that was going to cost, but Johnny had just gotten paid, and the overtime he'd been working had started showing up on the check. It wasn't enough for something outrageous like a new TV or the new transmission that "my" car needed, but it was enough for some store brand potato chips, sour cream and onion dip, and a six-pack of cheap beer.

"Maybe if there's a magazine or paperback that looks interesting?" I ventured. "Nothing too expensive." Some of those magazines were twelve dollars an issue, and I had no idea who'd shell out that kind of cash. But if he was going to have people over in the house, I was going to need my own entertainment, since I couldn't exactly leave. I had no idea who Johnny's "guys" were—I assumed his coworkers, and I'd only ever met one of them, briefly, when he gave Johnny a ride one week when we were waiting for the paycheck deposit to clear before we could buy a tank of gas.

That also meant I needed to get the kitchen and living room as presentable as they could be. It wasn't fancy, and there was no way it could be, but it could be clean. Otherwise it made me look bad. What kind of woman let her man's friends come over to a dirty house?

"All right." Johnny looked relieved, and I realized he'd expected me to fight him on it, to be angry. How could I be angry? Two weeks ago I'd expected that he'd be spending any time off with Jolene, or at least trying to. But instead he was here, fixing the antenna and having friends over to watch a baseball game.

I carved a smile out of the tense muscles in my jaw. "Thanks."

The house—or the parts of it guests would see, anyway—was mostly clean by the time Johnny got back. He'd bought two six-packs instead of one and a vegetable tray in addition to the chips and dip, but I swallowed the way that made me want to want to count the pennies in our change jar. It was fine. Maybe he knew he was getting more overtime coming up.

I tried not to crane to see if he'd managed to bring me anything to read—maybe that had been sacrificed to the grocery gods—but on one of my nervous passes through the kitchen, he reached into the bottom of the paper bag and came out with a paperback.

"Here," he said awkwardly, holding it out like he'd never held a book before in his life. "I wasn't sure what to get you, so I asked the lady at the register what she'd recommend."

Danielle Steele, the cover said. Well, all right. I'd never read any of her work, but I guessed they probably didn't have the kind of strange, obscure things I liked on the paperback rack at the grocery store.

(*A pale afternoon in the dead of winter, Cole sitting in the kids' section of the library with his feet up on the block-and-puzzle table, pretending to doze off in boredom while I sorted through endless racks of titles I'd never heard of two aisles away, opening the covers and checking the lending cards before putting them back on the shelf.*

"What are you doing?"

"Looking for which one hasn't been checked out for the longest."

A long groan. "Just pick one. By the time you're done, I'm gonna have to pay a late fee on mine.")

I set the paperback down on the end table beside Johnny's recliner and thanked him as I finished hefting the last laundry-basketful of clutter out of the living room and toward our bedroom. Maybe I'd take it outside with a glass of tea and read on the back porch while Johnny and his "guys" shouted plays at the screen or whatever.

But while I was moving a pair of Johnny's socks from the clutter basket to the hamper, I heard them arriving. The screen door creaked endlessly, like the drawn-out groan of an older brother in a library, and I could hear Johnny's voice, still low and measured but sounding more excited than I'd heard in a while. I stood at the foot of the bed with the basket braced against my hip, wondering if I dared go out to grab the book I'd left in the living room, or if it was too late now.

I didn't know these men. I wasn't wearing anything especially nice; I hadn't done anything to my hair or put a drop of makeup on. Would they pick on him for having an ugly girlfriend? I rubbed the knuckles of my right hand against my hip, stomach fluttering. Would they say anything about my hand? About any of the scars still visible on my neck and face, the notch in my earlobe? *They wouldn't say anything about Jolene.* Beautiful, perfect Jolene.

"Lil!"

Ah, shit.

"Lil, you left your book!"

"Coming!"

Two men I didn't recognize at all were standing around the living room while Johnny handed out cans of beer, along with the one I vaguely remembered having picked him up for work that one time.

I tried to sneak into the living room, but I had to pass through the corner of the kitchen to get there, and the tallest one flashed a warm, friendly smile my way.

"You must be Lilly Ann. We've heard so much about you. I'm Kevin."

"Hi." I managed to smile and wave with my left hand. "I'll be out of the way in a minute."

"Sure you don't want to stay and watch the game with us?" He didn't quite wink, but the rakish air was there. I smiled; it reminded me a bit of Cole, the way he was always trying to cajole or charm or sweet-talk somebody into something.

"No, but thanks for asking."

"Lil, you want anything to eat?" Johnny was tense, frowning, and I couldn't tell why. Was it because I was talking to his friends? Was I embarrassing him?

"I'm not hungry." I had no idea if I was hungry or not, but I sure as hell wasn't going to try to carry a plate of anything along with the book I scooped up off the end table. That would involve bringing way more attention to the right side of my body than I was comfortable with. Flustered and unbalanced, I didn't even think twice about opening the drawer in the table and palming the scuffed yellow box of fortune cards. "Have fun watching the game."

"Enjoy your book!" That from Kevin, bright and cheerful, and the other two guys laughed. Shit, I probably *was* embarrassing Johnny.

As I ducked into the bedroom, before I quite closed the door, I heard one of the men—not Kevin—say, "That's Cole Guthrie's little sister, isn't it?"

I paused. Had they known Cole, maybe in high school? It was a small town, so everyone knew vaguely of each other, but maybe they'd been friends of some kind?

"Yeah," Johnny grunted in response, and didn't elaborate. *Sorry, I'm sorry, I didn't mean to—*

A third voice: "Huh. I never really hung out with him, but he always seemed like kind of a fa..."

Something fell over with a clatter; dead silence followed. After a moment, Johnny said flatly, "Sorry, what was that you were saying about Cole?"

"Oh, uh—that he seemed like a...a fun guy?"

Pulse thundering, I pushed the bedroom door all the way closed. Johnny had a secondhand Walkman in the closet somewhere; maybe it still had batteries in it. Maybe it still had a cassette tape in it. I didn't want to spend my evening eavesdropping, guessing at what they weren't saying.

The Walkman was on a shelf in the closet. Batteries, yes; tape, no. It was my own fault; I'd just put all the tapes back in the living room while I was cleaning up. Maybe there was one in the back bedroom that served as the graveyard for anything Johnny wasn't willing to throw or give away. It probably wouldn't be a very good one, but it wouldn't have Van Morrison on it, either, which was more than I could say with any certainty about any of the FM stations I could pick up.

I eased the bedroom door open so nobody would hear and ask me what I was doing. It was the first time in a while I'd wished that I wasn't afraid of driving a car, just so I didn't have to worry about sneaking around my own house. The pop of the opening door was lost under male laughter, and a guardian angel must've put his finger on the hinges to keep them from creaking. The guys were all running their mouths anyway.

"Oh hey, I heard your cousin is back in town, Wade. She seein' anybody these days? Cause I wouldn't mind seein' a whole lot of her, if you know what I mean."

"*Dude.*"

"What? I know you're related, but you ain't blind."

I had one foot in the hallway when I heard something that brought me to a full stop.

"You forget whose table you're sittin' at?"

"Oh shit, Johnny." A laugh hit my ears like rubbing a cat's fur backwards. "Sorry, forgot you dated her. You get me though, right? You planning on trying to start something while she's here?"

I'd rather hear an hour-long marathon of Van Morrison than whatever Johnny was going to say next. The door clicked softly closed. The worn foam of the headphones caught on my ears as I fumbled them on. The radio switch flicked on to static, but the tuner rolled easily under my fingertips, past station IDs and commercials—"*...listening to ninety-one-nine FM, your family...*" "*...opening soon at Village Fair...*" "*...that was Miss Emmylou...*"—until I found a relatively clear signal claiming to be current hits only.

There was still a ball of anxiety rolling around in my stomach, knocking loose all the thoughts I'd worked so hard to pack up over the past few days. But that was why I'd brought the cards. Just to shuffle, I promised myself. Just for the feeling of it. I wasn't going to pull any cards, and I wasn't going to hope—not really, not head-on—that a handful would fall out like they had last time.

And, stubbornly obedient, the cards stayed in my hands. No messages from Miss Agnes or Cole or anyone else. Just...cards.

Despite myself, it did calm me, the familiar weight of their worn edges tapping against my palms. The radio was turned up loud enough I could only hear periodic bursts of voices from the living room, and it wasn't until my breathing started to slow that I realized how close I'd been to the edge of panic.

I turned the cards face-up in my hand, gently sifting through them, taking a moment to look at the illustrations. The familiar Magician, the stoic Emperor, the stern High Priestess.

The Lovers. A man and a woman, naked, with distance between them. I stared at the card and tried to imagine it with two women instead—Jolene and her...roommate—and then blushed. It felt wrong to insert her into the picture, and suddenly I realized exactly why I'd been so disgusted with the man who'd been speaking about her so crassly earlier. Maybe five years ago, or even two weeks ago, I wouldn't have thought twice about it. She'd earned her reputation after all, hadn't she? She was the one who had chosen to be that kind of girl. Promiscuous.

But I knew better now.

"Maybe I was trying to convince myself."

What would I have done in her place? Would I have tried to erase the desire for another woman's touch by any means necessary? Would I have looked for proof that the feelings weren't real, that I could close my eyes and imagine that a man's hands belonged to someone else? What if I liked him enough as a person; if we were good enough friends? Maybe I wouldn't have recognized the longing for what it was because I didn't know there was any other way to be—like I wouldn't have known before Jolene told me. Was that how it had been for her?

Deep in the deck, well past the Lovers, was the Star. Slowly, guiltily, I slid the edge of the card until it covered the male Lover, until the naked woman kneeling under a starry sky was staring across the celestial pool at the female Lover.

If I'd ever known how to breathe, I couldn't remember it now. My hand trembled as I stared at them. If this was the world Jolene lived in now, if this was the face love wore for her, she must feel as alone as I ever had as a shy, gawky child who would have given anything to step through a maze or a coat closet or a mirror pane to find another world, a place that understood me.

No wonder she'd made that face when I'd invited her to stay. No wonder she'd looked back over her shoulder as she left. If everyone in town knew—and thanks to Maggie Jean, they must—she probably didn't have a lot of people asking her over for dinner with the family.

I scooped the cards gently back into their box, closing the flimsy flap almost reverently, their whispers a small golden orb that rattled in my chest like a little lost sun that didn't know whether it was rising or setting.

EIGHT

IT STAYED THERE FOR DAYS, DESPITE MY ATTEMPTS TO IGNORE it, cover it, or push it away, reminding me that there were other worlds out there than what I knew—worlds that other people lived in every day. Worlds that were so different from the one I was in that they might as well have been on another planet entirely.

But this one was fine. It was enough. Maybe it wasn't the life I'd dreamed of as a child, but I had a roof over my head and food to eat, and Johnny took his promise to care for me very seriously. And maybe that's all there was between us, but maybe that was okay. How many times had I heard Beth and Donna talk about barely tolerating their husbands? At least Johnny and I never fought. As far as living arrangements went, it could be worse.

Maybe I could have been happy somewhere else—but maybe I would be happier not to lose my comfortable, well-worn existence... which was why I definitely didn't feel an excited little flip in my stomach on a Thursday afternoon when a loud, diesel-engine pickup truck rumbled up into my yard and Jolene hopped out of the driver's side with a varsity jacket slung across her arm. The colors of the Gideon High Bloodhounds, faded but recognizable, jolted me like a frayed cord in a live outlet.

I hadn't been to a football game since before Cole graduated, but he had been in the marching band and Johnny had been on the team, so I'd spent plenty of Friday nights perched on the uncomfortable aluminum bleachers, reading a book instead of paying attention to the score. Just the sight of that jacket brought back the exact taste of the concession stand's cheap chili dogs and the sound of the crowd singing along to the marching band's rendition of *You ain't nothin' but a hound dog,* and I opened the door before Jolene could even knock.

"You're home," Jolene blurted out, frozen with one foot on the front steps, and I realized she didn't know. She didn't know that I never left my house, that seeing me at her great-aunt's funeral had been a fluke, a combination of social obligation and needing to evaluate a threat. Unlike everyone else in town, she didn't look at me and see a shell of a girl hollowed out by grief, broken even on my best days.

I found I didn't want to change that.

"Yeah, that's my car." I pointed to the Chrysler up on blocks beside the driveway, clearly not going anywhere anytime soon. "Johnny takes the other car to work."

"Well, I was just going to leave this inside the screen door if you weren't home, but probably better that you're here." She held the jacket out to me, and I took it automatically.

"Probably," I agreed, shaking it out to take a look at it. "That screen door doesn't latch the best."

Meadows was stitched neatly on the front in silky gold embroidery, vibrant despite the streaks of sun bleaching across the deep purple fabric sleeves and the cracks in the aging cream-colored leather.

"This is Johnny's?" It seemed like an obvious question, but the real question was underlying: *Why did you still have it?*

"It was in the truck when I left town, and I wasn't going to come all the way back just to return it, but it didn't feel right to get rid of it. The more time passed, the worse I felt for having it, and the more I just... ignored it." She shrugged and gestured to it haltingly before stuffing her hands into her jeans pockets. "But you know, now I'm in town, so...no reason to keep it."

Despite myself, a deep suspicion settled into my stomach. Had she been bringing this by when she didn't think I'd be home, hoping to catch Johnny alone? Had the whole lesbi…*I like girls*…thing been to throw me off so I wouldn't suspect her real plans?

But if she'd been lying about that, she was a damn good actress, because I remembered the desperate fear in the press of her lips, in the white crease of her knuckles, in the welling tears dampening her eyelashes.

"Also—" Her voice broke my reverie, and I looked up from the jacket to see her pulling one hand out of her jeans, her fingers tightly curled around something. "I found this in the pocket of the jacket and…thought you might want it."

When she opened her hand, there was a huge bronze ring, slightly tarnished, with a bright aquamarine stone blinking from the center. I recognized it instantly.

"Cole's class ring," I breathed, holding my palm out. Jolene tipped it into my hand; it was still warm from hers. "Thank you."

Her smile was as bright as the sun that had broken through the storm last time she'd been at my house. "You're welcome. I'm glad I could give it to you."

"I'm gonna go put the jacket up," I said, and then because it was the polite thing to say, not because I didn't want her to leave yet: "Do you wanna come in?"

"Sure." She bit her lip. "But I was thinking, since your car isn't working, do you need me to take you anywhere?"

A cold sweat broke out across the back of my neck. "Oh…no, I wouldn't want to put you out." Thank goodness for manners.

"It's no trouble." She shrugged. "I've got a truck with a full tank of gas and nowhere else to be this afternoon. Do you need to run any errands? Want to get lunch or an ice cream—my treat?"

A refusal to the reissued invitation would be rude. It would mean that I specifically didn't want to go anywhere with *her*, because I didn't like her, and I didn't want to have accepted her kindness. I might as well slap her face. The only excuse I had left was how much I hated being in a car, and I still didn't want her to know that. I had made it to Miss Agnes's funeral and back, hadn't I? Maybe I could make it to wherever Jolene wanted to take me without her noticing I was secretly having a breakdown.

I clutched the jacket in one hand and Cole's ring in the other and took a deep breath.

"Okay."

Climbing up into Jolene's truck felt like climbing a mountain, for more reasons than one. I was short of breath by the time I clambered up onto the vinyl seat, and my hands were trembling as I latched the seatbelt.

"Sorry," Jolene said as she hopped into the driver's seat effortlessly. "It can be hard to get up if you aren't used to the height."

The truck roared to life when she turned the keys, and she reached to bump the radio volume down a bit but didn't turn it off.

"*...back with Mississippi's Top 40 and More after this break.*"

She paused a moment with her hand on the gear shift, looking over to check on me, but not the same way Johnny did. Not to see if I was hyperventilating or crying or passing out, but just to be sure I had my seatbelt fastened and was reasonably prepared for the vehicle to move.

I wasn't, but I gave her my best reassuring smile. If we sat here waiting for me to be ready, we'd never leave.

The radio commercials filled the cab between us down the red dirt driveway, and I tried to focus on them to keep the panic at bay. Instead of watching the scenery pass—watching for a flash of antlers or white tail coming over the ditch—I picked out a small, spidery crack in the upper right corner of the windshield, likely caused by a pebble thrown up by someone else's tires, and stared at it, gaze roaming around the strings of the glass web.

I don't know when the voice I heard stopped being a commercial for discount diamonds and started being Jolene. Maybe when she turned the radio down even more and said, "I won't hurt you, you know."

Her voice was small, both wounded and wound so tightly in on itself that it almost hurt to hear it.

I tore my eyes away from the cracked windshield and met hers instead as she braked for a stop sign.

"What?"

"You don't have to worry about being alone with me. I'm not going to take advantage of you."

The extent to which the thought had never entered my mind nearly knocked the wind out of me. Was it because I still didn't understand how women could be sexual with each other—oh, the glowing heat in my cheeks just thinking it—or was it because I trusted Jolene? And either way, did that make me a naive child, just asking to be taken advantage of? My mother probably would have thought it did, but my mother had seen danger lurking in every shadow sometimes. *And look what good it did her.*

"Oh, no, I didn't—" I shook my head. "I didn't think you would. I was…" I was what? Trying to keep from having a shaking, crying meltdown in your front seat? So wrapped up in my own problems that I forgot you were even here? "Just trying to remember if I'd left the oven on. But I didn't. I turned it off."

She relaxed a little, but I couldn't tell if she really believed me.

"It would really suck for you to go to all the trouble of bringing Johnny's varsity jacket back just to burn it up in a house fire because I forgot the oven was on."

I saw the moment she realized I was joking. I saw the confused knit of her brows untangle, her perfect lips part to let an unguarded laugh past her slightly crooked teeth, and a hint of pride welled up in my chest. I'd made her laugh. I'd created a feeling other than pity in another human. In *her.*

"Well, let's go have an ice cream to celebrate you not burning the house down," she said, and pulled out onto the main road.

I hadn't been to the Dairy Maid Treats-n-Eats since the day Johnny bought me an ice cream bar and invited me to move in with him, and I hadn't seen the girl behind the cash register since high school, before the accident. She turned toward the door as we came in, and I almost jumped behind Jolene when she shrieked, "Lilly Ann! I ain't seen you in a month of Sundays!"

Thank goodness for name tags.

"Hi, Tammy. It's good to see you." I was surprised anyone bothered to remember me enough to be excited to see me, but through all of middle and high school, Tammy had never been very popular. She'd been ignored and picked on by turn, like me, except without a big brother to look out for her. I'd been polite to her—not friendly, to my memory, but we'd sat together at lunch a couple of times and I'd never said anything mean to her. I guess that counted for something.

"...in here the other day, and she was telling me she saw you in town for that funeral a couple of weeks ago, but before that we weren't sure if you'd moved away, maybe. But listen at me, goin' on. What are you havin' to eat?"

"Oh, uh." I glanced over at Jolene. I didn't have any money with me, I realized. I hadn't stopped to get my purse or my pocketbook or even any cash on the way out of the house, and I didn't want to presume. "Nothing for me, thanks."

"It's on me," Jolene said. "I invited you, after all. Get whatever you want."

Nothing on the menu cost more than three dollars, but Johnny and I had been penny-pinching for so long, *whatever you want* was a foreign concept, so it felt a little heady to order a chocolate shake and fries while Jolene got a strawberry soda and onion rings. She held out a ten-dollar bill, but Tammy turned away to check on the kitchen. Jolene hesitated but set the money down on the counter instead.

"It'll be just a second," Tammy told me as she picked up the cash and punched numbers into her register. "Kitchen's dropping a fresh batch of fries for you."

Jolene held her hand out for the change, then drew back as Tammy dropped the quarters and pennies on top of the dollar bills and pushed the pile across the laminate counter.

And maybe Tammy hadn't meant anything by it, but I saw the hint of color on the bridge of Jolene's nose, the downturned corners of her mouth, and I replayed the last few minutes in my head. Tammy hadn't ever made eye contact with Jolene, hadn't interacted directly with her at all. Maybe the whole money-on-the-counter thing had just been a coincidence of convenience and timing. And sure, Jolene hadn't been in Tammy's grade at school and maybe she just didn't have much to say to someone she didn't know, but put together, it seemed...pointed. Or maybe, like my mother, I was just seeing problems that weren't there.

The longer we waited in complete silence, though, the more I knew I was right.

Jolene knew it too. Once our order was up, she didn't seem keen on sitting at one of the booths to consume our treats, so I followed her back out to the truck.

"Sorry she was rude to you," I said quietly as we were buckling our seat belts, and Jolene froze.

"Oh, I don't think she was...*rude*," Jolene said helplessly, but we were both from this town. We both knew complete strangers would tell you their life story at the drop of a hat whether you wanted them to or not. Not being spoken to, being ignored, meant that someone, somewhere, for some reason, had decided you didn't belong. "She was practically polite compared to some of what I've heard before."

I shook my head, but she wasn't wrong. Between the rumor mill while she was at school and the shock that had accompanied her return, she'd probably heard some things nasty enough that being ignored felt like a relief. But still—

"You don't deserve that. Not any of it."

For the second time that day, I'd surprised her. But instead of laughter like before, this time her face melted into soft gratitude, her eyes bright as emeralds, and I imagined what it must have been like to be Johnny Meadows in 1989, to lean in and kiss her.

It must have been divine.

* * *

The wooden picnic table tucked under a crooked grove of wide-spreading trees near the back of the park was deeply scarred with carved initials of couples that maybe were still together and maybe weren't. The playground swings creaking gently in the breeze several yards away had been new when I was a child but had spots of rust speckling the chains now. It was the middle of a weekday; the park was empty, and we were alone. It was the same park where Johnny had offered to let me move in with him. The same table, actually, still dappled in lazy sunshine and canopied by a drapery of silver Spanish moss.

"Can I have one of your fries?"

The afternoon light picked out every soft freckle on Jolene's face like a galaxy, her eyes wide but a little hesitant above them, her voice almost shy.

"Yeah, of course." I pushed the small paper bag of fries toward her and watched from the moment she took one—Did she bite her nails? The jagged edges were unexpectedly charming on her elegant hands, both index fingers slightly curved inward at a fascinating angle—until she bit it in half, a crumb from her own onion rings clinging to the outside corner of her naturally pink lips. It had never taken someone so long to eat a french fry; I'd never wanted it to take longer.

She wordlessly offered me an onion ring in return; I shook my head. I had more fries than I could eat, and there hadn't been many rings by comparison. I didn't want to deprive her of the food she'd paid for.

"It's funny you eat yours plain," she mused after a moment. "Johnny—"

She cut herself off with a guilty, nervous look, but I smiled. "Covers his in ketchup," I finished for her. Some people were dippers; some people were drizzlers. Johnny was a drowner, upending an entire bottle on his fries if given the chance. Even Cole had made fun of him for it.

"Cole used to ask him if he wanted some fries with his ketchup," Jolene snickered, and I felt my smile grow wider as she echoed my own thoughts. "But then Crystal got me hooked on dipping them in milkshakes."

"*In* the milkshake?" It sounded gross at first, but I was already having them together, wasn't I? I don't know what possessed me to pop the plastic lid off my cup and tilt it so that the mostly melted shake was accessible. Maybe I was starved for a new, novel experience; maybe I desperately wanted to impress her. Either way, I grabbed one of the fries, dragged it through the ice cream, then popped it in my mouth without hesitation.

Salt and sugar exploded in my mouth; hot and cold chased each other through my senses, crunching between my teeth and slipping across my tongue.

"*Oh.*"

"Good, right?" Jolene said, sounding as eager for my approval as I felt for hers.

I tilted the cup toward her and gestured to the fries. She only balked for a moment before she took the offer, and then she didn't hesitate at all.

My dad used to say that food tastes better when it's shared, and for the first time, I understood the profound truth of the greeting-card sentiment. I would never have another meal that tasted this good, no matter how many chocolate milkshakes and french fries I consumed. At that moment, I wondered if I'd truly tasted anything at all in the past five years.

When we were done, my fingers sticky from the milkshake and Jolene's lips bright red from her strawberry soda, she hooked a thumb toward the swing set and tilted her head.

"Wanna?"

And for some reason—*I knew the reason*—yeah, I really did want to. She started kicking herself toward the sky while I was still climbing into the curved rubber seat, shrieking giggles as she stretched out. Her hair fanned out, sweeping the dirt and grass as she see-sawed herself to greater and greater heights, but she didn't seem to mind at all.

I pushed myself slowly back and forth, toes never really leaving the ground. I wasn't sure I *could* swing that way anymore, with only one hand that would reliably wrap around the chain to keep me steady and pull me back up. It was enough to watch her fly, bright and shining, sparking like the edges of a remembered fire.

But even that didn't last, her dirty white Keds turning even grayer when she dug her heels into the dirt and jolted to a stop beside me. She opened her mouth, then glanced at my right hand resting on the chain, and I saw her go from quizzical to determined in an instant.

"Want me to push you?"

It wasn't a question, and she didn't wait for me to answer it before she hopped out of her swing and came to stand behind mine.

"No, I—"

She leaned in close, and her breath stirred the hair at the back of my neck as she murmured, "Point your toes and hold on. I got you."

I swallowed the suddenly dry protest that stuck in my throat, and I pointed my toes. And with Jolene's hands burning through my shirt all the way to my back…I flew.

Gravity paused at the top of every arc, leaving me weightless in a breathlessly blue sky, both more unchained from and more at home in my body than I'd ever been in my life. And when it swept me back down to earth, Jolene caught me every time, strong and gentle and just waiting to launch me back into the heavens.

I was still staggering and dizzy, my wind-tangled hair a stubborn riot around my face, when I finally climbed back into Jolene's truck, the red rays of the setting sun soaking through the whole world until there were no colors left anymore.

Jolene fished a pair of scratched Wayfarer sunglasses out of the flimsy cupholder under the radio and slipped them on. "Want a pair?" she asked, gesturing to the aviators that had been keeping them company.

It felt rude to accept but ruder to refuse, so I picked them up and flicked them open with one hand before pushing them onto my face. It had just been the more efficient movement considering the limitations of my right hand, but Jolene flashed me a crooked, crimson grin and said, "*Nice*," and she could probably see my blush through the sunset.

I snapped my seatbelt into its latch and sat back, amazed and grateful that just being in the cab of the truck wasn't giving me panic attacks. Maybe, I rationalized, because it sat higher off the ground than my parents' sedan or Johnny's Sunfire. Maybe, I thought as the diesel engine rumbled to life under the dented hood, it just *felt* different; maybe my subconscious reasoned that it was so tall there was no way a deer could leap from an embankment and come straight through the windshield—

"Lilly?" Jolene's voice was pitched in such a way that by the time I heard it, I knew she'd called me more than once. "Are you all right, hon?"

I blinked rapidly until I saw where I was—in the intact cab of Jolene's truck, the redness in my eyes from the sunset and not from a cut above my eyebrow dripping down into my face, nothing but slightly torn vinyl covering the seat next to me, no shattered glass—and tried to control myself, but I was already faint from not breathing, and the less air each gasp pulled in, the more frantic the next one was until I could see darkness at the edges of my vision, my head swimming.

I was dimly aware of Jolene turning the truck off and flinging her seatbelt to the side to scoot across the bench seat toward me.

"Whoa, whoa—breathe, honey, breathe," she coaxed, catching my left hand between both of hers and pressing her thumb into the hollow of my palm, grounding me. "Breathe with me, okay? We're gonna count. Breathe in until we get to five. One, two... Nope, keep breathing in, one more time."

Finally I was able to focus on her voice, on her face so close to mine, counting me to five, then holding for three, and then exhaling until my lungs were emptied of air and the metallic taste of an impending collapse.

We did it three more times until I was breathing normally again, and when she gradually released my hand, I felt the ghosts of her fingerprints lingering on my skin like fog on a windowpane.

"Are you okay?" she prodded softly, and somehow I knew she was only really referring to whether the immediate crisis had passed, but I also felt like I owed her an explanation. I thought of her small voice, her sad eyes when she'd thought I was afraid of being alone with her, and I ached at the thought that she might still think that.

"It's... I have trouble being in a car, sometimes," I said, the words still shaky. "I have... I guess it's flashbacks?" I wet my lips to try to steady myself. "To the...the accident."

"Oh my God." She reached for me again but stopped herself halfway, her hand falling to the seat between us. "I'm so sorry, I didn't even think about—You could've—I'm so sorry I didn't ask. We don't have to drive home. We can walk. We can find a bicycle. Hell, I think Crystal's rollerblades are still in the toolbox."

The absurd mental image of me tottering down the road on rollerblades while Jolene tried to steady me—or pull me behind herself on a bicycle—was what finally brought me all the way back to myself with a wobbly smile.

"No, I'll manage," I promised her. "Thank you for...getting me through it."

She peered at me through her sideswept bangs. "You're sure? Like, *sure*-sure? I don't mind walking you home."

I swallowed hard, my throat tight. No one else in my entire life had ever treated me like this, except maybe sometimes Cole. I was the quiet one, the one who just went along. I brought a book with me everywhere because I could choose where I sent my mind while my body waited outside a dressing room or in a restaurant booth or on somebody's couch with their cat.

But Jolene was not only giving me the choice, she was giving me time and space to make it. She wanted to be sure I was doing what I wanted, not what I thought she wanted me to want. And she believed that I could handle it.

"I'm sure-sure." She deserved full honesty, though, so—"It might still happen again. I can't control it. But I'll try to tell you before it gets to be too much, all right?"

That seemed good enough for her. She relaxed and slid back under the wheel, slotting her seatbelt into place. "All right," she agreed, adjusting the Wayfarers back onto her face. And even though I couldn't see her eyes anymore, I knew the exact shape and color of them when she said, "Tell me if you need *anything*, okay? Anything at all."

And I promised I would, even though at that moment I had no idea what I needed.

NINE

JOHNNY'S CAR WASN'T YET IN THE DRIVEWAY WHEN JOLENE pulled into the front yard, and I found I was grateful not to have to explain to him where I'd been or with whom. I hadn't been doing anything wrong—*right?*—but somehow it felt like I had.

"You'll be okay by yourself?" Jolene asked, peering at the dark trailer as I unbuckled and shouldered open the heavy truck door.

"Yeah. Johnny should be home soon." Halfway out of the truck, I realized she'd be alone too, and nobody would be there to be sure she got home safe. "Um, if you…" Maybe it wasn't my place. Maybe it was too demanding. But I knew part of me would wonder if something had gone wrong the minute she was out of sight, and I also knew that she deserved to feel like someone in this town cared about what happened to her. "If you remember, when you get home, do you mind calling to let me know you got there safely?"

A tiny twitch of a smile. "Yeah. I can do that." The smile was still there when she glanced up in the rearview mirror at the end of the driveway and gave a little wave before pulling away.

It wasn't until twenty minutes later, when I heard Johnny's car crunching up the driveway as I was running water into a pot, that I remembered she told me that she still hadn't gotten the telephone situation figured out at her apartment. Maybe she'd forgotten about that, too.

"Hey." Johnny's voice at the entry of the kitchen made me turn to see him. He already had his shirt off, smudges of grease and dirt and oil on his arms and jaw. He looked so tired; too tired for someone who had just been in high school a few years ago. I looked at him for a long time, wondering if Jolene would recognize him now. If Cole would. "What's for dinner?"

"Spaghetti." Easy to cook, easy to clean. "And garlic toast."

He nodded. "Sounds good. I'm gonna shower." He'd only gotten a few steps down the hall when I heard him stop. "Hey, where'd you find this?"

His letter jacket. I'd forgotten about it already. "Oh." I didn't consciously decide to lie; it just rolled off my tongue. "I found it while I was cleaning out the closet."

I wasn't proud of that fib, but I also wasn't ready to deal with how Johnny might react to hearing that Jolene had come out to the house. Maybe Jolene had moved on, but that didn't mean Johnny had. How could he? I'd just spent several hours with her, and I already knew I'd never be quite the same. He'd been with her for two years.

He was silent as he rubbed his thumb over the embroidery of his name, and he didn't say anything else as he dropped the jacket back to the recliner where I'd left it. The next thing I heard was the shower coming on, and I turned back to the pot of salted water and unopened jar of Prego.

Cole's class ring was still in the pocket where I'd put it so I wouldn't lose it. I should get that. Maybe Johnny wouldn't care, or maybe he'd appreciate the sentimental reminder, but I hadn't had enough time to sit with my feelings about it yet. I couldn't face up to his.

The water wasn't yet boiling, the oven still heating up for the toast, so I took a minute to go fish the heavy piece of metal and brightly colored glass out of the jacket—the jacket that smelled like Jolene. I hadn't realized it before I'd spent the afternoon with her, but there was a lingering air of sunshine and dust and a floral echo that clung to it, and when I smelled it, I could see her smile.

Surely I was imagining things. I lifted the fabric to my nose without consciously deciding to, Cole's ring slipping into the nest of my palm—and then clattering to the floor and underneath the recliner when the phone jangled, my nerves ringing louder than the bell. I stared at the faded beige plastic contraption, imagining the worst, imagining Aunt Pauline on the other end—*Heard you been around town with that Jezebel, shoulda known if there was a puddle of sin you'd find a way to jump into it*—but I scooped it up with a "Hello" that almost passed for normal.

"Lilly?"

Oh—! "Jolene!"

"Sorry, I hope I didn't disturb you. I just wanted to… Well, I told you I'd call you to let you know I got home, and I got home, so—"

"You're not bothering me at all. After you left I remembered your phone wasn't working. Did they get it fixed, then?"

"Oh, uh." She laughed almost nervously, and I heard the sound of tires whirring past in the background. "No, I walked down to the payphone at the gas station."

I knew where Miss Agnes's apartment was, and I knew where the convenience store with the payphone was. They weren't very close. "Jo…" My voice failed completely. "You didn't have to do that."

An engine revved in the distance. "I didn't want you to worry. I feel bad about…putting you through all that, with the truck and the flashbacks…"

"Well, thank you." The shower shut off and the raucous bubbling of the water in the kitchen pressed on my eardrums; I suddenly remembered I wasn't the only person in the house and Jolene wasn't the only other person in the world. "I, uh, gotta go. Supper's on the stove, and the water's about to boil over, but—"

"Yeah, yeah, of course! I don't mean to keep you. Have a good night."

Johnny's hair dryer whirred to life in the bathroom, buying me a few more seconds.

"Hey, Jolene?" I waited to see if I'd caught her in time; there was no dial tone, just breathing on the other end. "Do you maybe…want to come over again? In a few days? If you have time?"

A laugh as soft as the smile I'd last seen on her face. "I'd love to."

And this time there was a click. This time there was a dial tone, and I dropped the receiver back into the sticky cradle before I dashed back into the kitchen to rescue the spaghetti. Heat down, noodles in the pot, and my hands only shook a little as I got the saucepan onto the other eye.

The dryer stopped. Johnny walked like he was trying to stomp the foundation further into the earth, but it was just how he'd always moved—on the football team, he'd been the guy who planted his feet and made himself a brick wall for the other team to break themselves against. Cole had spent a whole afternoon one time trying to knock him down for the hell of it. Now the trailer trembled as he came toward the kitchen, and the jar of Prego damn near vibrated off the counter.

I caught it, but barely, and braced it against my body to try to twist the top off.

"Were you talkin' to somebody?" he asked, holding out one hand for the jar. I gave it to him. The ends of his hair were still damp, swept across his forehead. "Thought I heard you."

"Oh, just—" The lid jolted open with a loud pop, and I jumped, wincing as a drop of tomato sauce landed on my cheek. "Just a wrong number."

"Huh." Johnny set the open jar down on the counter and reached for my face. I flinched. The boiling water bubbled and splashed, and the stove element ticked rapidly as it heated. His hand hung in the air where he'd been about to wipe the drop of pasta sauce off my skin.

"Sorry." I blushed and reached up to swipe at it myself. "Supper will be ready in a minute."

Johnny wasn't ever much of a talker, but dinner that night seemed quieter than normal, and I spent most of it trying not to squirm in my chair. More than once I thought about telling him about my afternoon, about swinging and ice cream and *Do you remember how Cole used to tease you for putting so much ketchup on your fries?*, but all the words bumped up against the knot of guilt in my chest and never made it to my mouth.

What if he got mad at me for spending time with Jolene? He'd been so hurt to see her at Miss Agnes's funeral, resentment simmering in him so loud I could almost hear it bubbling. In that light, my giddy afternoon was almost a betrayal, downright disloyal, and I was sure he'd see it that way too.

He scraped his plate clean, mopped up the leftover sauce with his garlic toast, and then looked over at my plate where I was still slowly twirling spaghetti around my fork, lost in thought.

"You good?"

"Oh." My stomach clenched at the thought of eating anything else, but wasting food was maybe the biggest sin in this house. It was too expensive to go scraping leftovers into the trash. "I'm not very hungry. Do you want the rest?"

He grunted. "Put it in the fridge. I'll take it for lunch tomorrow."

I found a plastic container and started packing up my leftovers plus what was left of the pasta and sauce, and he started clearing the dishes off the table, but suddenly the kitchen seemed too small for both of us, his elbows and feet taking up all the breathing room around me.

"I'll finish the dishes," I blurted out, both hands clenched on the plastic lid, the pinch of the rough edge grounding me. "You've been working all day."

"You sure?" But he was already wiping his hands off, stepping back from the sink. I nodded, and I saw the strange, jerky motion when he almost leaned in toward me but stopped himself. I stared down at the little wet kisses of steam dying against the container lid. "G'night," he said, and I think I muttered something similar in return.

I took my time cleaning the kitchen, wiping up stains that had been there for years—some maybe even longer than I had—hidden in little corners easily missed by the usual cleaning instruments. Around midnight, I had to admit that I was just avoiding going to bed.

I thought about sleeping on the couch but if I was honest about it, I was always a bit unnerved by the blank, silent television. I put on a soft nightshirt and eased onto the edge of the mattress, doing my best not to wake him. His back was to me; he was facing the wall, his arms folded over his chest. His breath caught on a snort as I settled onto my pillow, but he didn't stir more than that, and I closed my eyes and prayed that I'd be asleep before he woke up.

* * *

I don't know when I managed to drift off, but I must have because I was dreaming of flying—of falling—when the sound of shattering glass yanked me upright into consciousness. Johnny was beside me, still facing the wall, still snoring quietly. He'd always slept like a stone. Cole had told me Johnny could sleep anywhere at the drop of a hat. *"Even in the middle of a conversation."*

I reached for his shoulder to wake him, then thought better of it. What if the sound had just been in the dream? I didn't hear anything else, no footsteps or objects moving. If someone had broken into our house, what were they going to get? A busted TV, a cigarette-pocked off-brand recliner?

Still, I knew I wasn't going to be able to sleep if I didn't see for myself. I crept silently out of the bedroom, wishing like hell that Johnny had played baseball instead of football and that there was a bat nearby I could grab.

Hell, who was I kidding? Even I'd had a bat, the likelihood of my being able to knock out an intruder by swinging it at his head was slim to none. There was a grim sort of zen to that realization, and I rounded the end of the hall into the living room half prepared to tell an intruder to kindly make sure the screen door latched securely behind him when he left.

But the room was empty. Awash in glowing moonlight, but empty. No strange shadows, nothing moving, nothing out of place. A quick jiggle of the handle reassured me that the door was still locked. The kitchen was next; maybe I'd left the sauce jar on the countertop and it had finally fallen after all.

No. Nothing.

"Think I might be finally losing my mind, Cole," I whispered aloud, pushing my hair out of my face. As if in answer, a pale blue light winked at me from under the edge of the recliner—Cole's class ring, where I'd dropped it when Jolene called. The metal was warmer than I expected when I scooped it up but still cool as I closed my fist around it, the engraved numbers of his birthdate scraping against my skin, reminding me.

It was almost September; Cole's birthday, always the first party of the school year, was right around the corner. I always baked a special little cake—vanilla with cherries and cherry icing, his favorite—but I hadn't been to the cemetery since right after the memorial service. Maybe I'd try to go this year. Maybe I'd ask Johnny to take me, if he didn't have to work. I wished I could ask Jolene, but her lack of a telephone was the least of the reasons I couldn't.

"I'll come see you," I told the ring. "And Mom and Dad." I set the heavy piece of jewelry down on the table beside the recliner and turned back down the hall. But instead of creeping back onto the mattress with Johnny, I opened the door to the junk room instead. There was an old daybed that had belonged to Johnny's sister before she'd gotten married and moved to Hattiesburg; it still had a quilt on it and a couple of pillows, and if there was a fine layer of dust on top of the stack of vinyl albums and winter clothes, well, that just meant the bed underneath them should be fairly clean.

Removing everything felt too purposeful, too permanent, so I just moved enough to be able to crawl into the empty space between the wall and the crate of Beatles and Bob Dylan and the Jimi Hendrix Experience. If Johnny asked why the next day, I'd tell him I hadn't wanted to wake him up, but in the meantime, having my own space— even one barely big enough for my body, carved out of literal junk piles —felt like a kind of freedom I hadn't known I'd been craving. Like swinging; like strawberry soda; like freckles and french fries and flying. I curled my fingers into the holes of the plastic crate and enjoyed the rough cardstock edges that greeted me on my way past them into deep, sound sleep.

Ten

On the first day of September, the birdsong in the woods behind Johnny's trailer shifted. It was still swelteringly hot, still summer in all the ways that counted, but to me and the birds, September had arrived. Johnny's friend Wade was having a cookout for Labor Day weekend, and apparently Kevin had been put in charge of calling to tell us. I'd answered the phone, and while I told him we'd *think about it,* he did his best to sweeten the deal, offering to pick us up in his truck and bring a book from his bookshelves at home for me.

"I don't know what's there aside from an Encyclopedia Britannica and maybe some car repair manuals, but you're welcome to bring your own, too. Hell, I'll run to the library before they close tonight if you want."

"What did you tell them about me?" I asked when I hung up. "Kevin seemed to think he had to talk me into letting you go. He even offered to get me a book from the library."

Johnny frowned. "He shouldn't be teasing you," he muttered, but I shrugged.

"I don't think he meant anything by it." I didn't want to come between Johnny and his friends just because he thought he had to wrap me in bubble wrap. I could handle being poked fun at once in a while, even if I couldn't handle the idea of going to a backyard cookout with strangers and their wives. I wasn't up to that level of performance. "I think he's just trying to be friendly. I think you should go. I'll bake you a pie to take with you."

If Johnny had been at all surprised at the implication that he'd be going by himself, he didn't mention it.

I had a five-pound bag full of discount apples with spots and bruises, and since Tuesday would be the first day of school, I probably wouldn't have as many pie customers, so Saturday morning saw me making the fanciest apple pies I knew how to make. I might not be making an appearance, but maybe at least the latticed flag on one and star on the other might impress the suburban housewives enough that they wouldn't judge me for not accompanying my man.

I was peeling a Granny Smith and carefully carving the bruise out of it when the phone rang. Johnny was watching television in the living room, so I expected him to answer it. When it rang a third time, however, I paused and called out to him.

"Johnny? Are you going to get that?"

There was a brief moment I thought maybe he'd fallen asleep in his recliner before he responded, "...Get what, Lil?"

I huffed, but it didn't ring again. Whoever was on the other end had given up, I guessed. The answering machine hadn't even stirred.

"Taking a nap?" I tried to keep the annoyance out of my voice. If it was important, the person would call back. Hopefully it wouldn't be Wade or Kevin telling us the party had been canceled. I didn't want to go, but I was a good halfway through baking. I had to admit I was looking forward to hearing any compliments my pies might garner— and it would be good for Johnny to get out and socialize without having to worry about me.

I wondered if they'd invited Jolene. Wasn't she Wade's cousin? I hoped the other women wouldn't be too cruel to her. What if Johnny was the only friendly, familiar face at the barbecue for her? The only person she could talk to? I didn't particularly think Jolene wanted Johnny back, but I couldn't blame him if he still wanted her. If seeing her reminded him of what he'd once had, and drew a stark contrast between us. What if he decided he deserved better, and maybe Wade or someone else had another cousin who would be perfectly happy to give that to him? Would I be devastated or just…relieved?

"What did you want me to get?"

Johnny's voice in the kitchen doorway startled me and the paring knife slipped, apple juice stinging instantly as the blade bit into the webbing between my thumb and forefinger.

"The phone." I snatched a paper towel to staunch the bleeding, the knife clattering into the sink. "It's stopped now, though."

Johnny eased further into the kitchen, taking my hand and turning on the running water in the sink. "The phone wasn't ringing, Lilly Ann."

I caught my breath as he stuck my hand under the water, both from the sting and the implication.

"It rang three times," I argued. "I heard it."

"It didn't ring at all." His grip on my hand was tight, too tight. Little droplets of blood squeezed up through the cut.

"Stop." I tried to pull my hand back. "I've got it. I can take care of it."

He didn't let go, his brows knitting together as he held me there. "What's gotten into you lately? You've been acting strange."

I finally pushed his hands off mine, wet the paper towel, and turned the water off. "Nothing," I said, holding the wet towel to the cut. "I'm fine."

The blood slowly spiderwebbed through the fibers, the spreading pink blob making my heart pound as much as the white lie did. I was *fine,* if "fine" meant questioning my entire existence instead of just feeling my way through the same fog everyday.

I'd learned to do a lot of things left-handed after the accident; would I have still cut myself if I'd been holding the knife in a whole right hand instead? Would I still be in Gideon if my mother was alive to insist I ought to go to college? Would my life be different if Cole was still around to tell me to go find out what I wanted instead of cowering in a trailer, afraid to lose what I had?

Would I still be obsessed with Jolene if she weren't the symbol of everything I'd never been and always wanted to be?

"If you say so."

But the moment he turned from me, the phone *did* ring. My eyes snapped to him to see if he was hearing it too; had I really lost my mind?

But he was picking up the receiver, saying hello, and I breathed a sigh of relief. Not crazy after all. Not like that, at least.

"Hello?" he said again. "Anybody there?" The phone clattered back into the cradle and he snorted. "Guess they didn't want to talk to me. If you're gonna start being psychic, though, could you at least tell me what numbers to play in the lottery?"

The joke was its own kind of apology, and the weak smile I gave him in response was my own kind of acceptance. "I'll do my best."

"I'm headed out to the shop," he said. "Told Wade I'd bring some briquettes and Grandpa's old grill in case he needed a backup. Gonna get it ready before Kevin comes by."

He was out the back door and I was elbow deep in the medicine cabinet before I realized what he'd just admitted. He hadn't talked to Wade after Kevin had called the day before, which meant he'd already known about the cookout. He'd already been invited, by himself, and had been planning to go. He'd clearly told the guys that I wouldn't want to come, and that was why Kevin had called to invite me, specifically. Nevermind that Johnny was right about whether I'd want to go; what had he been planning to tell me? That he'd be working?

My hands shook as I put antibiotic ointment and a bandage over the cut on my hand. How often had his long hours at work actually been him spending time with his friends instead? Was that why, despite hours and hours of overtime, we never seemed to get ahead financially? Johnny always handled the checkbook. I didn't contribute much to our bank account, so it seemed reasonable that he'd be the one to pay attention to where the money went—but that meant that I actually had no idea what had been on his past few paychecks.

It was a strange revelation. No, I wouldn't have wanted to go anywhere if he'd invited me, but why had he felt he couldn't even tell me? Did he feel guilty about being social and enjoying himself while I was sitting at home alone, the personification of a small, anxious dog who couldn't go for car rides?

Suddenly I knew that no matter how nice my pies were, it wouldn't influence how anyone at that cookout thought about me. They already knew. I was always going to be that poor Guthrie girl who was never quite the same again after her whole family died, *bless her heart*, isn't it sweet that Johnny sacrifices so much to give her a place to stay? She can't be giving him what he needs in a relationship—so sad, what a waste, he's so handsome, he could have anyone he wanted—

The phone rang again and I nearly jumped out of my skin. Was there something going on? Was the phone company testing the lines? When I answered it, though, there was someone on the other end.

"Lilly! Hi, I'm not interrupting anything, am I?"

Jolene.

I was smiling from the moment she said my name.

"No, not really." Just an ongoing existential crisis, apparently, but there was no use waiting for that to be over. "Are you okay?"

"Oh—yes, I'm fine, thank you. I just got the phone turned back on at Aunt Agnes's. I wanted to check to see if it was working. I mean, I called the Time & Temperature, but I wanted to be sure…"

She didn't say as much, but I'd already realized it the night Johnny's friends had come over to watch the game. I was the only person she had to call.

"That's great," I said cheerfully. "That you got it working, I mean."

"Yeah, so I—I wanted to give you the number, too. In case you need anything. Since you don't have a car." There was something in the cadence of her voice that made me think she must be pacing as she talked, and I couldn't help but be endeared.

"Thank you, that's sweet of you. Let me get a pen to write it down." I had to set the phone down; there wasn't a pen or paper anywhere within reach of the cord. I didn't want a piece of paper that could be easily lost, either, or that I would have to leave sitting out where Johnny might see. For whatever reason, I still didn't want him talking to Jolene.

The Danielle Steele book had some blank pages in the back that worked just fine, though. He wasn't likely to borrow that to read anytime soon. After I recorded her number, Jolene hung up, and I told myself I wasn't disappointed that she hadn't wanted to talk longer, that she hadn't asked if she could come over.

I finished baking the pies. Johnny finished cleaning up his grandfather's old grill just as Kevin's truck rumbled into our front yard.

"Those smell amazing," Kevin said as I handed over the pair of pies in their tin plates, covered with aluminum foil. I wasn't taking a chance on not getting my mother's nice glass plates returned to me. "Are you sure you don't want to come with us? There's room in the truck."

Up until that exact moment, I had absolutely no intention of going anywhere near that cookout, but something about knowing that Johnny had *planned* to go without me, and hadn't told me at all, was just planning to let everyone shake their heads and pity me, pity *him*—

"You're sure you don't mind?"

Johnny dropped the grill on his foot and swore, and Kevin turned toward him.

"Oh, hey buddy, let me help with that. Hang on."

Kevin helped me into the truck cab first, handing me the pies once I was settled, and then went back to the truck bed to help Johnny load up the grill. I sat in the center of the bench seat, feet primly on the hump in the floorboards, pies stacked neatly on my knees. At least Kevin's gear shift was attached to the steering wheel, like Jolene's, and not in the middle.

Oh God, what was I doing? I didn't belong at a barbecue with people who knew how to be normal. I wasn't even wearing anything decent—just cut off denim shorts and a white tee shirt, something lightweight to deal with the heat—and my hair was just up in a messy ponytail. Great plan, Lilly Ann. Show up looking like Rochester's wife escaped from her attic to prove to everyone that you haven't lost your mind.

I hadn't even brought my book to hide behind.

I couldn't do this. It was a mistake. I'd say I wasn't feeling well, I'd—

The doors on either side of the cab opened, and Kevin slid under the steering wheel, Johnny climbing into the passenger's seat more slowly, eyeing me with something like suspicion.

Well, I was trapped now.

I clung onto the pies as Kevin's truck rattled down the driveway, to the gravel side road, and then out onto the country highway beyond. I clenched my jaw to keep my teeth from chattering and stared straight ahead even though I could feel Johnny staring a hole in the side of my head. And when we passed the old white church with the oak-shaded cemetery that held the remains of my family, I had to close my eyes and count my breaths down the way Jolene had taught me.

"You okay?" Kevin asked, his voice a startling reminder that I existed in a space where other people could perceive me. This whole thing was off to a great start.

Johnny stirred beside me, but I spoke over him: "I just get a little carsick sometimes." As lies went, it was better than saying I'd left the oven on. It wasn't even *entirely* a lie, just a fib, as Cole used to say. Mom had always been charmed by his insistence they weren't the same, but Aunt Pauline had whipped him for it once when we were young. That was the last time Mom had left us alone with Aunt P, now that I thought of it.

"Well, hang in there, it's not too much farther to Wade's. Some cool air on your face might help." Kevin reached for the air vent, and my heart jumped into my throat the second his hand left the steering wheel.

"I got it," I blurted out, leaning forward to adjust the air vent myself. It did help a little, actually, the cold air drying out my eyes. The aluminum foil on the pie plates crinkled loudly as I settled back against the seat, and I sent up a prayer to whoever might be listening that I lasted through this afternoon.

* * *

Wade's house was a modest little brick ranch-style, nothing too fancy, but the minute we stepped into his backyard, I understood why he was the one hosting the cookout. The lawn sprawled out for what felt like forever before it hit the neat privacy fence, and the neat, green grass had been set up with horseshoes, a bean bag toss, and a slip 'n slide with a sprinkler at one end. Several very wet children were flinging themselves down the bright orange strip of vinyl with carefree abandon while their parents lounged in lawn chairs with red plastic cups.

"Johnny!" Wade called out. "You're just in time! Bring that grill over here. We're gonna load it up with these babies." He kicked a wicker basket, and out spilled bright green ears of corn, the cream-colored silk quivering like satin tassels.

"Oh, that's our cue," a woman I didn't recognize drawled, tilting back her bottle of light beer before she headed across the lawn to pick up the basket of corn. By what seemed to be unspoken consent, all the women adjusted their lawn chairs into a semicircle, and the corn basket was placed in the middle, along with a metal bucket. "With all of us working together, we ought to have it all husked by the time the menfolk get the grill heated up."

Because it was more awkward to stand alone doing nothing, I eased into the circle and claimed an armful of ears for myself. I sat on the grass and lost myself to the steady, methodical motions of peeling back the green husks, tying them with wet twine, and carefully stripping out the cornsilk from the kernels while conversation flowed around me.

"...converting the guest room into a third bedroom for Mandie. She's turning fifteen soon, and she's been asking forever to have her own room so she doesn't have to share with her little sister."

"But tell them the real reason, Joanna."

"Okay, fine, it was so Wade couldn't ask me to let his cousin stay with us."

I froze, fumbling the wet twine I'd just picked up. Surely Wade had more than one cousin—but the women's laughter told me no, it was Jolene Whitaker they were talking about.

"I thought she was staying in Mrs. Randall's apartment?"

Joanna made a face as she tossed a stripped corncob into the metal bucket. "The lease is only prepaid through the end of

September, and from what Wade tells me, there's some kind of legal holdup with Mrs. Randall's will." She leaned in like she was imparting a secret, although the volume of her voice didn't change at all. "They're trying to keep from causing a scene, but we think what's really happening is that her mother is refusing to release her portion of the inheritance. Something about her reflecting badly on the family."

A murmur ran through the circle; several tongues were clucked.

"She's always reflected badly on her family, if you ask me. What's changed now?"

I felt sick to my stomach, the cornsilk clinging to my hands as I tried to peel it away.

"I'm not one to gossip," Joanna said, holding one hand up as if in a plea for understanding. "But my understanding is she got involved in some *real* disgusting, sinful things when she left town after high school. Still, I don't think it's right to deny the last wishes of the dead. I say let her have the money."

The first woman, the one who'd dug for the gossip in the first place, laughed, and it was an ugly sound. "You just want her to have the money so she has a place to stay that isn't your house."

"And can you blame me?" Joanna sat back and started working on the next ear of corn. "Let he who is without sin cast the first stone and all, but what kind of a mother would I be to let her in my house with two impressionable daughters?"

That was all I could take. I put my one clean ear into the bucket, dropped the rest back into the basket, and blurted out, "Can I use your restroom, please?"

All the women looked up at me, startled, as if they hadn't noticed me at all until that moment.

"Oh—of course, honey. If you go in through the back door, head down the hall to your right and it's the second door. You can't miss it."

As I fled, my stomach roiling, I heard one of them whisper, "Who was that?" and I could have laughed if I hadn't been so angry. I hadn't even needed to come; they didn't care about me. They wouldn't have said anything. They would've eaten my pies and said terrible things about one of the nicest people I'd ever met and never would have spared a thought for me at all.

And what did I care if they did? I'd never seen these women before, and if there was a God in heaven, I never would again. It didn't matter what they thought or said about me. And it shouldn't have mattered what they thought or said about Jolene, but there was a bright crack of anger down the seam of the shell I'd built around my feelings five years ago to keep from drowning in my own sorrow.

Jolene had barely known me. I was the orphaned younger sister of her ex-boyfriend's dead best friend. I was living with her ex-boyfriend. But the first words she'd spoken to me had been kind, and she had reached into the darkness time and again to find me when I couldn't find myself. She didn't deserve to be ignored like Tammy had, and she sure as hell didn't deserve to be spoken about like that, especially by someone who was family, however far removed.

How many of those women would talk about their husbands the way Jolene had talked about the woman she'd loved? Maybe one or two, but I knew the rest of them. Maybe not personally, but I'd known women like them my whole life. They'd picked a man they could settle for because they'd wanted to be wives and mothers. And maybe they were happy. Maybe having a husband's paycheck and a husband's house was worth the exchange of their time, their attention, their bodies.

Hadn't it been enough for me too, in my own way?

My hands shook as I washed them in the bathroom sink. I dropped the pink, shell-shaped soap more than once, and when I finally got it back in its ceramic dish, I realized that it had taken my bandaid with it.

I carefully wrapped the cloth in a bit of tissue and tucked it into the small, pristine trash can beside the toilet. No one wanted a gross, bloody bandage from a stranger just lying around their bathroom after all. I was, however, not going to feel guilty about rummaging through the cabinets and linen closet to find a fresh one. Maybe my aunt or my mother might have scolded me and told me it was more polite to ask my hostess, but my hostess could go jump in a lake.

By the time I'd gotten a new bandage securely on my hand, I'd calmed down enough to try to figure out how I was going to survive the rest of the afternoon. I couldn't just ask to be taken home—maybe if Johnny had driven me, but I couldn't impose on Kevin. I could insert myself into the men's social circle instead, but that was enough of a faux pas that it might actually cause a scene.

My only option, it seemed, was to stand vaguely near the kids' play area in a way that could be excused as keeping an eye on them to be sure nothing got out of hand or earned a trip to the emergency room. At least there wasn't a pool and there weren't darts involved—the culprits of both of Cole's ER trips. Even the horseshoes looked to be made out of plastic.

I didn't know how long I'd been standing there when a red plastic cup materialized in front of me. I took it reflexively, looking up to see who had brought it to me, and was both surprised and not to see Johnny frowning out at the kids on the slip 'n slide, holding his own cup.

"Somebody's going to break their neck on that thing," he said idly, and I snorted.

"I was just thinking at least it's safer than a pool with a diving board."

"Maybe." He sounded unconvinced, but his body language seemed relaxed. "You doing okay? I really didn't think you'd want to come."

Was it an admission, an apology? I couldn't tell. And hell, at this point, I was done being mad at him anyway. He'd done what he thought was best. I knew him well enough to know that. He'd known the kind of people who would be here and had correctly surmised that they weren't mine. It left the question: Were they *his* kind of people? Or could he just put up with their company to have someone to spend time with who wasn't me?

"Kind of regretting it, if I'm honest," I admitted, and he nodded. That was clearly the answer he'd been expecting. "Don't know what possessed me."

"Do you want me to tell Kevin you've got a migraine, see if we can drop you off back at home?"

It was an offer as sweet as the tea in my cup and one I was very tempted by, but I could stick it out a while longer. Probably. "Maybe after dinner," I conceded. "That silver queen corn looked like it was going to be delicious once it's grilled." I tried on a smile; it fit better than I expected. "I managed to husk one entire ear before I chickened out of the conversation, so I feel like I'm entitled to eat that one, at least."

Johnny huffed a laugh and shook his head as he took a sip out of his cup. For a long moment, he just watched the kids playing and didn't say anything else—but just as I was going to tell him he didn't have to worry about me, he could go spend time with his friends, he spoke.

"You know, Lilly Ann... You deserve to be happy."

I blinked. "What...do you mean?"

He shrugged, tight and uncomfortable, and took a long drink from his cup. "I don't know. But if there's something that makes you happy, you don't have to give it up. Not for me, not for your family. Being happy doesn't mean that your pain wasn't or isn't real. You don't have to be miserable to prove you loved them."

I couldn't have closed my mouth if I'd wanted to; the hinge of my jaw was too loose, the muscles too slack with shock. Before I was done even comprehending the words he'd spoken, much less what they meant, he pointed to the red and blue bean bags stacked on the grass in front of a couple of targets.

"Wanna play?"

I couldn't think of a good reason to say no, so I said yes—but I spent the rest of the night turning his words over and over in my head like a puzzle box.

What possible happiness did he think I was denying myself? By the time Kevin dropped us off at the doublewide, I was no closer to figuring it out than I had been when he'd first said it—and it wasn't until he was sound asleep that I realized I should have said, *You do too.*

Eleven

Cole's birthday was scorching hot, but it tapered into a crisp evening. Johnny was quiet when he got home from work and went to bed before the sky was fully dark, leaving me awake and as restless as the fireflies dancing under a lopsided moon.

You deserve to be happy, Lilly Ann.

His words from Wade's cookout the week before still haunted me. I'd spent long hours peering closely at the elements of my life, trying to find what had made him say that—and failing. What would make me happy? Well, right now, telling my brother happy birthday. I'd baked his cherry-vanilla cake, just a little one, and put it in the fridge. I'd been planning to ask Johnny if he wanted to share it with me, maybe talk about Cole. It had been so nice to hear Jolene's stories about him, and I thought maybe Johnny would appreciate a similar freedom.

I hardly knew what I was doing when I slipped Johnny's car keys off the key rack by the door. The silver Sunfire was in the driveway, and although the night was quiet, I knew Johnny would sleep through the sound of the engine starting. Only the thought of getting myself stranded gave me pause, a metallic scent wafting up from the keys in my sweaty hand.

They made a gentle clattering sound when I dropped them on the scratched little table beside the cigarette-scarred recliner, a little scrape when the phone cord bumped them out of the way. I opened the Danielle Steele book just to double check, but I knew the number by heart without ever having dialed it.

I held my breath as it rang; was it too late to call? The last gasp of twilight framed the trees against a lighter sky, but night was falling fast. Just when I was second guessing myself, lowering the receiver away from my ear, the ringer stopped. A soft click, and then—

"Hello?"

Her voice sounded muffled, almost stuffy, and I winced. "Jolene? Hi, it's Lilly. I'm sorry, did I wake you up?"

A sniff, a deep breath. "No, no, I'm awake. Are you okay? What's wrong?"

"It's…" I couldn't. There was no way I could ask her. She was dealing with so much already, if half of what Wade's wife had said was true. "It's nothing. I'm sorry. I shouldn't have called. Good night."

"Lil—" Her voice was so sharp as she spoke over me that I froze, my left hand tight around the receiver. I heard her take a shaky breath, and her voice was as deep as the night when she said, "Don't—don't go. Why did you call?"

It took a huge effort to swallow my pride, but finally I admitted, "It's Cole's birthday. I was going to go to his grave, but…I can't drive. And Johnny's asleep."

"I can take you." She hadn't even hesitated. "I'll be over there in ten minutes."

"No, Jolene, I can't ask—"

"You aren't asking; I'm offering."

My throat tightened on a wave of emotion, but I nodded. Then, realizing she couldn't hear that, I murmured, "Thank you."

"I'll see you in a minute."

I waited at the edge of the yard; maybe if she didn't pull all the way up, the truck wouldn't wake Johnny. My stomach felt like all the fireflies from the back woods had taken up residence just under my diaphragm—quiet little aimless flutters, uncertain glowing blinks, long stretches of darkness as they fumbled helplessly toward an instinct they didn't understand. I was on my feet the second I saw the soft orange gleam of Jolene's parking lights—she didn't have the headlights on, as wary as I was of waking Johnny.

I handed up the plastic-wrapped dish with Cole's cake on it, and Jolene took it without question. Once I'd clambered up into the seat and buckled in, she handed it back to me.

"Ready?" Her voice was pitched low, like we might somehow speak loud enough to bring Johnny out of a dead sleep when the truck engine hadn't. I nodded, clutching the plate.

"Ready."

She took a second to take the cassette out of the player, flip it to the other side, and push it back in before she popped the truck into gear and swung the front end into a wide U-turn. She turned the headlights on as soon as we were facing away from the trailer, casting sharp shadows through the trees.

I didn't know the song that started playing, but there was tape case on the seat beside me, so I tilted it to look at the cover. It had a blonde woman, her chin tilted up defiantly, the words *Yes I Am* boldly below her face. I thought I recognized her, but I couldn't remember exactly. I liked her voice, though, rough and tender all at once, electrifying in a way.

"This tape was Crystal's," Jolene said after a minute, with a crooked little smile. "But she left it in my truck when she packed her bags, so it's mine now."

"Are you okay?"

The question surprised even me, bursting past my lips without a conscious thought on my part.

"Me?" She glanced away from the road to my face once, twice, flexing her hands on the steering wheel. "I'm—yeah, I'm—Why do you ask?"

Unspoken was the observation, *You're the one visiting your dead family in the middle of the night. Which one of us is more likely to not be okay?*

"I just mean..." I shrugged. I didn't know whether to admit that I'd heard about her current troubles from a distant relative at a barbecue she hadn't been invited to. "It hasn't been that long since you broke up, right? And I figure it's not like a lot of people are asking you about it."

"Oh, that's…very kind of you." She swallowed hard. "I'm all right, though. On that front. At least…if I have any feelings about it, they're all just different shades of anger right now."

"I understand that," I murmured softly, thinking of how I'd sat and simmered in rage at my family's memorial service, and how it had been the only emotion I could face at the time.

It wasn't far to the old church, and Jolene pulled the truck around the back. As we approached the cemetery fence, I slowed, my shoulders drooping. The gates were locked. Of course they were. It closed at sunset.

"You coming?" Jolene said, several steps ahead of me at this point.

"It's locked."

"And?" She grinned. "Not *everything* they said about me in high school was a lie."

The chain link fence rattled as she tested it with her foot, and I looked around automatically, my heart pounding, like someone was going to find us.

"Can you climb over?" The tone of her question anticipated a *no*, and some stubborn part of me—the same part of me that had gotten into Kevin's truck, apparently—nodded.

"Yeah, I can."

Her eyebrows went up, but she took the cake from me and gestured to the fence.

"All right, up and over."

At least it was short. A wealthier church might have had a nicer fence, higher and harder to climb. Blessed are the poor, I guess. I managed to lever myself most of the way up, got my right leg over— and then my left foot stuck. The damn shoelace had gotten caught on a broken link.

"Oh, hang on." Jolene set the cake aside and came closer, bending near my leg. Her hands on my bare ankle above my shoe were shockingly warm, and I nearly toppled the rest of the way over, stuck foot or no.

"Whoa," she laughed. "How'd you even…? I'm gonna take your shoe off so you can get down. Hold steady."

She slipped my foot out of my canvas sneaker like a reverse Cinderella, then braced me by the hips as I got the rest of the way over and down onto the ground. The fireflies in my stomach weren't nearly so lazy now, zooming all over the place. My skin felt hot and too-tight, and I pressed my hands to my cheeks as she finished getting my shoe free and passed it over the fence to me.

The cake was next, and then while I sat down on the grass and put my shoe back on, she clambered over, lithe and nimble—and notably *not* getting anything stuck. "You know where you're going?"

The question refocused me sharply, but after a moment of looking around, I nodded. I hadn't come out here much after the funeral, but the location was burned into my memory. And anyway, it wasn't very far from my grandparents' graves, and my mother had brought me to leave them flowers several times.

She stayed with me until we found them, then shoved her hands into her pockets.

"I'll give you a minute, yeah?" She smiled. "Just yell if you need me."

Oh. "Okay. Thanks."

She wandered farther down the path, and I slowly sank down in front of the headstones. James Alan Guthrie, Susan Ezell Guthrie, Cole Aaron Guthrie. And beside Cole, an empty plot that would have been mine.

I curled my fingers into the cool green grass and closed my eyes, drawing in long breaths and exhaling them slowly. I felt myself crumbling from the inside out, stone walls washing away under an inexorable sorrow, a slow-rising tide of memory and emotion lapping at the shore of my consciousness.

I tasted salt before I knew I was crying; felt the grass on my face before I realized the weight of it all was too heavy to bear sitting up. I'd spent five years burying the details of that day, but now they were reaching up through the grave dirt and I couldn't pry their cold, bony fingers away.

I should have been paying attention instead of reading. I knew it was probably the last time I'd see my brother for at least a couple of years. Everyone else seemed so proud of him for joining the army—even my mother, who couldn't stop worrying out loud, and my father who told her every time that Bush wasn't Nixon, and that things were better now than they had been in Vietnam—but I just felt like I was being left behind.

Cole reached across the backseat and bumped the spine of the book in my lap, grinning when I scowled at him.

"Cheer up, sour puss," he said, pitching his voice low so as to not interrupt the argument our parents were having in the front seat. "I'll write you letters every day."

"I don't care about your dumb letters," I muttered back, kicking his ankle. "Besides, I bet you'll forget after the first six months anyway."

I expected Cole to keep teasing me, but he just watched me for a minute, his stare making it impossible to read the words on the pages I was holding. "What?"

"I know you want to get out too," he said quietly. "You'll get your chance. Maybe after high school."

"Oh yeah, cause Tuscaloosa is so far *out*." Despite myself, I would take what I could get. And if what I could get was a scholarship to the University of Alabama and a dorm room two hours away from our do-nothing town, then it was better than being stuck in Gideon until I died, like everyone else.

"You know you could go to college somewhere else," he said, but I didn't miss the cautious glance to the front seat to make sure Mom and Dad hadn't heard him. It wasn't like we could afford for me to go to college out of state, and he knew it as well as I did. He'd be all right, once he got back from deployment. The VA would pay for his college, and he could go wherever. Like he wouldn't have already been halfway around the world and seen more things than I could even dream of. Not under circumstances anyone would envy, of course, but it was an easier thing to focus on than the reason he was going.

"I don't even know if I want to go to college," I admitted. What would I major in? I didn't have any big, grand goals. I didn't want to build bridges or rocket ships, didn't want to teach kids or discover a cure for cancer. I just wanted to see what was out there.

"Not go to college?" my mom said from the front seat, inserting herself directly into the middle of our conversation. "Of course you will."

"She doesn't have to if she doesn't want to." My dad was right on her heels without missing a beat. "Right, pumpkin?"

"I just think she should be prepared," Mom muttered. Cole and I glanced at each other, because they weren't actually having a new argument now; they were just continuing the one they'd been having before, albeit with new words and topics. In the lull while all of us tried to figure out how to change the awkward subject, Van Morrison wailed on the radio about his brown-eyed girl, and my mom huffed and reached up to the change the station. "Hate this dumb song," she muttered, and Cole grinned at me.

He'd told me once that she hated it because it had been Dad's song with the girl he'd dated before Mom, and she never, ever let it play if it came on the radio.

"Aw, I like it," Dad complained. "Besides, Lil's got brown eyes. Don'tcha, Lil?" He looked up in the rearview mirror and winked at me, and I smiled back at him. "Anyway—"

"Jim, look out!"

Five years later, I still didn't know if I actually saw the deer's legs come through the windshield, or if I just knew they had because I heard Aunt Pauline talking about it at the funeral. I still couldn't tell if I actually remembered the moment the oncoming car spun into the passenger's side doors and trapped my hand in the metal, or if I just knew that's when my fingers were crushed so badly they had to be amputated later.

But I knew for sure that I never saw the moment Cole died, because when I had woken up in the hospital later, I'd asked where he was. Some part of me knew Dad was gone, and I remembered enough of my mother's shaky voice, the blood on her face, that I knew she was worse off than me even if she'd survived. But Cole... Where was Cole?

It still destroyed me that I didn't know the last instant I saw my brother. Was it the look we shared over Mom's distaste for Van Morrison? Was that really the last time I'd seen the one person in the world who seemed like he really *got* me, the one person who promised me I'd get out of Gideon someday if he had to drag me out himself?

I remembered that first panic attack wrenching a piercing alarm out of the heart monitor, and my frantic, shallow breathing that won me an oxygen mask shoved over my mouth and nose. And even though the sedative they injected into my IV made everything seem very quiet and very far away, it couldn't make me forget what they'd told me: I'd lost everyone. Just like that. No Dad, no Mom, no Cole. And honestly, although I wouldn't realize it until a year later when the anniversary of the accident came and went and everyone treated me like a broken doll while I valiantly tried to prove they didn't have to... no more me.

* * *

I lay there in the grass above my family's graves long enough that I finally stopped crying, and although my face hurt when I pushed myself back up to sitting, I felt clearer. I couldn't see Jolene from where I was, and it didn't feel right to yell across the quiet graveyard.

I tidied the headstones idly, brushing away little dead oak leaves and squirrel-chewed remains of pinecones and acorns. The silk flower arrangements that were there didn't look too weather-worn, which made me think maybe Aunt P had brought them by not long ago. The anniversary of the accident had been at the beginning of the summer; she'd probably come out then.

When there wasn't anything else left to tidy, I just sat with my knees tucked up to my chin and spilled out everything that had been on my mind for the past few weeks. We'd had our fights, as most siblings do, but Cole and I had always understood each other. We talked to each other about everything, and I knew he would have listened without judgment when I told him how much time I'd been spending thinking about Jolene.

"I know you know how nice she is," I said. "You liked her, even though you were jealous that Johnny spent so much time with her. I remember how mad you were when they started dating, but then the three of you went everywhere together."

We'd even all gone to see *Labyrinth* together, before Johnny and Jolene were an item. At the time, I hadn't realized that Cole and I had been crashing what Johnny had probably intended to be a date, or at least an attempt at one. I was a kid and just wanted to see the movie. Cole and I had both been obsessed with it; I think we went to see it every weekend it was in the theater. I wondered now if Jolene remembered that time, how we'd sat in the row behind them and Cole had spent the first half of the movie throwing popcorn at the back of Johnny's head. I remembered now that she'd gone to the bathroom right before the ballroom scene, and when she'd come back it had been to find Cole in her seat. She hadn't seemed flustered at all, had just come to sit beside me with a friendly smile.

The twelve-year-old that I'd been hadn't cared at all who was in the seat beside me. I'd just been fixated on the spectacle onscreen. At the time, I'd ignored her, but now I wondered what she'd thought of it all —the movie, Cole inserting himself into their date, Johnny letting him. Maybe I'd ask her, assuming I ever found her again. Where had she gotten off to? The cemetery wasn't *that* big.

I stood up, knocking grass and dirt off my legs, and peered around. The moon was bright, but the cemetery was shaded, giant oaks spreading their canopy over the sky, just letting a dappling of light drip through onto the grass. It definitely wasn't enough to see very far.

"Jo?" I wet my lips; unless she was close by, she hadn't heard that. I tried again, a bit louder: "Jolene?"

It was strange to realize how empty and how dark a stretch of land full of the dead and buried could be in the middle of the night when you couldn't find the other person you'd come with—and yet, not silent. Rustling leaves, crickets, frogs, the occasional nightbird trilling or hooting all sounded louder than seemed possible, almost overwhelming. Past the edges of the cemetery, in the thick of the trees, I thought I saw a bobbing, erratic light, and my pulse kicked up.

It's just the fireflies, I told myself. Will-o-the-wisps didn't exist, or if they did, they weren't ghosts.

But if there was ever a place a ghost might feel welcome to roam, a semi-abandoned cemetery in the middle of a warm summer night seemed like the perfect candidate. I felt a tug in the center of my chest, as if someone had hooked a string around the bone there and was reeling me toward the forest, toward the light...

A twig snapped behind me.

I screamed.

So did Jolene—who, it turned out, was the twig-snapping culprit.

"Oh my God, you couldn't have said hello or somethin'?" I snapped, hand pressed to my chest to try to keep my heart behind my ribs.

"I did," she insisted. "You looked like you didn't hear me. Are you okay? I saw you just standing here..."

She'd seen me? She'd called out to me?

"I guess I was distracted. I was watching this light..." I turned, gesturing toward the woods, but there was nothing there now. No fireflies, no soft moonlight, no floating supernatural gleam. Just a dark, quiet forest, all the creatures temporarily frightened into silence by the ruckus we'd made.

But with Jolene beside me now, the eerie atmosphere seemed dispelled. It had just been my imagination, nerves from being the only living person in a graveyard at night.

"Do you need another minute?" Jolene asked now. "I can go—"

"No!" I laughed nervously. "No, no, I'm done. But do you..." I hesitated. "Do you want to help me eat Cole's birthday cake before we go?"

I wasn't sure what reaction I expected from her, but it wasn't the soft, affectionate smile she directed toward my brother's headstone.

"Actually, yeah," she murmured. As we sat on the grass and I unwrapped the cake, she mused, "His birthday party was something we all looked forward to every year. My parents and I moved up from Mobile when I was seven, and I didn't know anybody at school, but Cole invited the whole class, including me. He was friendly to me when no one else was."

"That was Cole," I agreed with a little smile. "Mom always used to say he could make friends with a fencepost. Total opposite of me."

I thought I'd brought two forks, but there was only one on the plate. Maybe the other one had fallen out when we'd been climbing the fence.

"We can just share," Jolene said after I'd been fruitlessly searching for the other fork for a few minutes. "Just pass it back and forth."

Oh God. There wasn't a good reason for me to say no, but oh boy did my stomach do a somersault when I said yes.

When there were only crumbs left, we both said goodbye to my family and headed back toward the truck. Jo helped me climb the fence again—no getting stuck this time, but no wayward fork visible nearby either—and then held a flower out to me as we walked. I looked around to see where she'd gotten it from, but it was a sprig of night-blooming jasmine that was growing on a section of the fence. It smelled divine.

"I appreciate you inviting me out here," she murmured. "I felt bad that I hadn't gotten to tell him goodbye. He was a good friend." I took the flower hesitantly, and she smiled. "You are too, you know."

And just like that, she'd turned me into the one doing her a favor instead of the other way around. I took a deep sniff of the jasmine and accepted that she'd outmaneuvered me on this one.

"You're welcome."

Twelve

"What's this?"

I looked up from the cardboard box in front of me, its lid discarded onto the dusty daybed. "Stuff Aunt Pauline packed up for me when they sold the house." I hadn't actually gone through it at all in five years. There were three boxes total—which didn't seem like a lot, for a family of four in a decent size house—and even the thought of peeling off the packing tape and peeking inside had filled me with panic.

This box, the first one I'd opened, had an eclectic mix of personal belongings. Among a bunch of old magazines and framed photographs, I'd found my dad's reading glasses, my mother's favorite brooch, and what I had in my hands: Cole's yearbook.

It was open to the spread on the school's sports teams. Basketball, baseball, and of course, the school's pride and joy, the football team. The large black and white photograph that covered one whole page of the two-page spread showed the marching band at halftime for the homecoming game, the team all lined up behind them. I could just see the edge of Cole's snare drum and the epaulets on his shoulder in this photograph. He'd loved the showmanship inherent in being the snare drummer.

"If you spent half as much time on your homework as you spend throwing drumsticks in the air and trying to catch them, you'd have straight As," our father had complained more than once.

Farther back was the team, and Johnny must have been with them, but I couldn't spot him in this photograph. Across the box from me, though, he was frowning, shoving a baseball cap onto his head like it had personally insulted his mother.

"Well, don't just leave it out when you're done," he grumbled, and I stared at him across the page. When I didn't say anything, he rubbed the back of his neck and left the room. He was back a second later.

"Boss offered me and Wade a chance at some good money," he said, hands shoved deep in his pockets. "Friend of his is a contractor out in Meridian, needs a couple of welders to work overnight. Tonight. The pay is..." He shook his head, blowing out a breath. "The pay's enough to finish fixing your car, and maybe somethin' else. Who knows."

"Oh." I closed Cole's yearbook. "All right. You'll be back tomorrow?"

"Yeah. They're getting us a hotel room to crash after we get off shift, so we'll be home around noon." He scratched almost anxiously at his stomach. "You don't sound mad. You'll be okay by yourself?"

I thought about it. Maybe a few months ago, I would've quailed at the idea, but now it didn't seem like a big deal. How many days had I barely even seen him at all because he worked so late he'd just come home and gone straight to bed? It wouldn't be any different than that.

Except that he wouldn't be here *at all*. Despite myself, a half-formed thought was already sending up sparks of excitement: With Johnny gone, I could invite Jolene over. Heck, she could stay as long as she wanted.

"No, I'll be fine."

He nodded slowly. "All right. Wade'll be by to get me about five o'clock. We can fit more of our tools in his truck, so..."

"Okay. I'll pack you a lunch to take with you."

It was the longest four and a half hours of my life. Johnny took a nap, I packed a few sandwiches and two mini-pies in a paper bag for him, and then finally, as the afternoon sun stretched orange fingers through the trailer, I heard tires in the driveway.

"Thanks for the food," Johnny said from the top step by the door.

"Tell Wade I said hello," I said politely. "I packed you two little pies, so you can share if you want to."

I waited until they were well out of sight, and then a few minutes more, before I headed toward the phone. Even as I dialed and listened to it ring, I kept one ear out for the sound of Wade's truck coming back, in case Johnny had forgotten something, but it didn't. Jolene didn't pick up, either.

Hmm. Maybe she wasn't home. Disappointing, but I could try again later. No sooner had I slipped the receiver back into its cradle than it trilled, jump-starting my heart with a burst of adrenaline and—felt strange to admit, even to myself, but—hope.

"Hello?"

A quiet sniffle. "Lilly?"

I sat down hard in the recliner beside the phone. "Jo? What's wrong?"

"Sorry, I…" I heard her trying to steady her breathing, the way I always had trouble with after a crying fit. Something about your lungs taking longer than anything else to realize the danger is past. "I don't mean to impose. Is…um, is Johnny home?"

"No, he's out overnight." I frowned; did she want to talk to Johnny? Was he—

"Oh, good. Can I… Can I come over?"

It was such an impolite request, made so hesitantly but with such relief, that I knew something was very, very wrong.

"Yes, of course. Now?"

"N-now. Yes. Thank you."

Waiting for Johnny to leave had been interminable torture; waiting for Jolene to arrive had me wanting to crawl out of my skin. I don't know why I chose to pass the time the same way—by packing food into little paper bags. Mom had always baked when she was anxious or upset; I didn't have time to bake anything, but I could sure put together a decent cold supper of fruit and cheese and beef jerky and a couple of Little Debbie cakes. Two thermoses, one with water and one with sweet iced tea, were screwed tightly shut and set beside the lunch bags.

I was at the door the second I heard the truck engine, still most of the way down the driveway. I flipped the porch light on and stood out on the top step, watching as she parked beside Johnny's car and got out of the cab. I could tell she had been crying before she'd taken two steps, and I acted without conscious thought, bare feet skimming over the cinderblocks and the dying late-summer grass until I was close enough to reach for her.

She came into my arms without hesitation, and I held her tight, my left hand spreading out over her shoulders, my right hand pressing her close. She hid her face against my shoulder and let out a strained, shaky breath. I felt the heat of fresh tears through the thin sleeve of my shirt, and I rubbed her back softly and made soothing noises, the same way my mother had done for me when I found out my soon-to-be-former best friend Ruby hadn't invited me to her birthday party in the fifth grade, or the way Cole had done when I'd gotten violently sick from drinking the ill-advised concoction we'd made of several leftover liquids in the fridge. The way I'd wished someone—anyone—would have done for me after the accident. After I lost my whole family.

Eventually her tears stopped and she let go of me, taking a half step back and using both her palms to wipe the wetness off her face, sniffling loudly.

"God, I'm so sorry," she said. "I don't know—"

"You don't have to be sorry." I caught her right hand with my left one and squeezed. "Do you want to go somewhere and talk about it?"

We probably could have talked about it inside, but I didn't want to. I'd been inside that house for five years. I liked going places with Jolene. I liked being in her truck and listening to her music. I liked seeing all the well-worn places in this dried-up, never-changing town like I was experiencing them for the first time. Maybe it made me a little selfish to ask, but I had a bribe:

"I have a couple of snack bags put together. We could find a picnic table somewhere."

Jolene nodded. "Do you mind if I come in and blow my nose while you get the bags? And then we can go."

I didn't mind at all. I got the bags and my shoes and—because I knew how crying doesn't stop once you get started—a box of tissues. I had no idea where she was taking me, but I didn't really care. There was a kind of flutter in my stomach, both like and unlike the nausea that usually sat there while I was in a moving car.

I vaguely recognized the general direction we were heading— toward the westside hunting lodge and one of the creeks that eventually flowed into the Tombigbee River on its way to Mobile Bay. She pulled over before the turnoff to the cabin, though, following a dirt road out into the middle of a hayfield that had already been harvested, big round bales sitting at regular intervals through the field. When she turned off the headlights, there was nothing but starlight and the hint of a waning moon to wash the wide-open field in a warm, blue glow.

Without a word, she dug a quilt out from behind the seat and headed toward the bed of the truck, letting the tailgate down with a loud metallic pop. I followed her with the bags of food and the thermoses, watching as she spread the quilt out over the bed of the truck.

We didn't speak; we just worked quietly in tandem as I handed up the picnic and then she reached back down to help me climb up. I kicked my shoes off to feel the sweet night breeze on my toes, and she sat down beside me and did the same. I handed her one of the bags and then held up both thermoses.

"This one has water, and this one has sweet tea," I said, and she pointed toward the water bottle. When I handed it to her, I noticed a large shadow on the side of her forehead, and I peered closer. "Is that —a bruise?"

"Oh, this?" She reached up to the spot and winced as soon as her fingertips touched it. "Apparently some asshole decided I was worth wasting a full can of beer on and threw it at me from the window of his buddy's truck."

"*What?*" I wasn't prepared for the instant flame of rage that licked over me. "Who was it?"

"I don't know," she admitted, and I believed her. "I didn't recognize him." She laughed bitterly. "Guess he recognized me, though."

"Jo, honey…" I couldn't help reaching for her face, and she let me, though I didn't touch the bruise, just hovered right above it. "When did that happen? Is that why you were crying?"

She snorted, opening her snack bag when I pulled my hand back. "You'd think so, right? No, being hit in the face with a beer can didn't make me cry, but talking to my mother sure as hell did." She heaved a sigh. "So I don't know if you've heard any of the gossip about Aunt Agnes's will."

"A little," I admitted. "Johnny works with your cousin Wade."

"Ah. So you know my mother has been withholding the money Aunt Agnes left me in her will. Apparently no one in the family understands why I in particular was singled out to receive a decent amount of cash and some of her jewelry."

I tilted my head; Miss Agnes had living children, grandchildren. Jolene was just her great-niece. I, too, desperately wanted to know why she'd been singled out, but it seemed rude to ask. Jolene must have known I was wondering, though. Or maybe she just wanted to talk about it.

"Aunt Agnes knew I was—am—queer. She figured it out, actually. I didn't have to tell her. It never changed how she treated me, though. I think she…" She sighed. "I don't know if she was queer herself, or if she just wanted to support me and knew what things can be like."

"Why doesn't your mom want you to have it?"

Jolene wrinkled her nose. "A lot of reasons, but it boils down to that she's punishing me for embarrassing her just by being alive. But without the money, I can't renew the lease on Aunt Agnes's apartment. I've been applying for jobs, but nobody's hiring, and even if I got hired tomorrow…they want first and last month's rent. I don't have that without the inheritance."

I remembered Wade's wife saying that she'd given her daughters separate bedrooms just so Wade couldn't offer their extra room to Jolene in a fit of familial compassion, and I assumed from the situation that the rest of her family must have been similarly inclined.

"Anyway. Tonight Mom said she'd give me the money if I promised to leave town and not come back or contact them until I—in her words—straightened myself out. So, never."

I sat bolt upright, the thermos of sweet tea rolling out of my lap and onto the truck bed with a loud thunk. At least the lid was still on. "What the hell! Jo! That's not fair!"

Jolene picked up the thermos and handed it back to me with a sad, bitter smile. "Fair or not, I don't really see another option." She opened her own thermos and took a long swallow of water. "It's not like I ever wanted to stay in Gideon. I just...didn't really expect to be thrown out."

I sat, shell-shocked, staring out at the looming hay bales. Just when I'd found something—someone—that made my prison tolerable. Just when I'd started finding myself again, even discovering new pieces of myself... To think that it was all going to be ripped away because her own family, her own mother, couldn't stand the thought that Jo liked to kiss girls instead of boys. What the hell! Who cared about that?

I twisted my thermos open with a bitter vengeance and took a swallow, but when I closed it again, Jolene caught at my hand. Butterflies surged from my stomach up into my throat, taking my heart with them.

"Are you bleeding?"

Oh. I blinked and looked back down at my hand. The scab from where I'd cut myself making the apple pies for that damn cookout had come off. "Oh, it's nothing." I held my hand up in the moonlight; just a tiny drop of blood sat on top of my skin. "It was almost healed anyway, I think."

"I've got a first aid kit behind the seat. Sit tight."

Well, what else could I do? I didn't want to get blood on the quilt. It was nice; seemed handmade. While Jolene clattered around in the cab of the truck, I rested my hand in my lap and tilted my head up, staring at the sky.

As I watched, a small streak of light zoomed across the zenith, and I caught my breath.

Make a wish, my brother's voice said in my head. What would I wish for? For Jolene to stay—and be miserable in a town where people ignored her to her face, threw beer cans at her, and bent over back-wards to keep from having to show her hospitality? I couldn't do that to her, no matter how much the thought of a future where I never saw her again seemed cold and bleak and empty.

Jolene came back with a bandaid and wrapped it very gently over the wound. While she wasn't looking at me, I murmured, "When are you leaving?"

"I don't know yet. I guess it depends on when my mother decides to give me the money. I haven't…told her that I would take it yet."

I flexed my hand when she was done, then blurted out, "I saw a shooting star a second ago."

"Oh yeah?" She hopped back up on the tailgate and looked up at the sky. "I think we're still in season for the Pleiades."

I reached for her without even noticing which hand it was. "Do you want to see if we can spot any more?"

Maybe with enough shooting stars, I'd finally figure out what to wish for. Jolene took my hand hesitantly, scooting back until we could lie down together, staring up at the dark sky without speaking.

The whole left side of my body felt like ice—probably just in comparison to the fire burning in the right side, where Jolene was pressed against me from shoulder to hip, her arm casually threaded through mine, her left hand resting on my wrist. She gasped and pointed every time a fleck of light streaked across the Milky Way that twinkled above us, and sometimes I even managed to watch the stars instead of the delicate shape of her hand, the rough edges of her bitten-off nails a charming flaw in her shining perfection.

How was I going to live without her?

When we hadn't seen any for almost two whole minutes, she tucked the quilt closer around the both of us, her voice as soft as honeysuckle on the night breeze. "You know about when stars fell on Alabama?"

Every schoolkid in Alabama knew about it. November 1833, a meteor shower that lit up the night like the noonday sun at the end of the world, like the return of a vengeful Christ, as the populace flung their vices into the closest flames and threw themselves to their knees to beg for mercy. *He has loosed the fateful lightning of his terrible, swift sword.*

I nodded. "Yeah."

"What would you do?"

Some part of me was distantly aware that I should have said I'd be with Johnny, but I couldn't. I also couldn't say what I really would have done. There was no one here to hear me except her, no one to judge me except myself. But if I said it aloud, it would be true, and I didn't know how to let it be true.

"I'd go to church, I guess." Church. To repent for the lie that tasted so bitter on my tongue, sour in my stomach. Because the terrifying truth was, if I thought I only had minutes to live, if I knew my actions would be free of consequences, what I would want more than anything in the world—

"I would find you."

My heart stopped beating. My breath stuck in my throat. Jolene lay there staring at me, into me, through me. There was no laugh to soften the blow of her words—because they had been hers, not mine, no matter how much I'd known the same in my heart. *The truth is marching on.*

She slipped her hand lower on my arm, across my wrist, over my palm, curling around the scarred, bony ridges, her pinky catching mine, her thumb rubbing over the rough edge of the bandaid there. My blood sang to the surface of my skin, flooding me with warmth, rising to her touch. She rolled onto her side and reached for me, the fingers that had been pointing to the stars now trembling over my face, down to my chin.

I said her name just to taste it on my tongue, then again as she leaned in close, a verbal surrender. When I tried to say it a third time, she stole the sound right out of my mouth, inhaling my voice and claiming it for her own.

My left hand was in her hair before I knew it, and I felt the noise she made as she shifted half on top of me, our quilt-cocoon beginning to swelter as my senses were flooded with the shape of her. And within that chrysalis, I felt myself melting, reshaping, *transfiguring* into a creature of pure desire, craving nothing but the warmth and glory of her skin against mine.

Beyond us, the sky was streaked with dizzy stars, but I didn't dare wish for anything.

THIRTEEN

The next day, having not slept at all for the giddy feeling in my stomach, I repacked all of my family's boxes again. I paused with Cole's yearbook, flipping through the pages to see if I could spot Jolene in any of the pictures. My face felt hot whenever I thought about her. We hadn't talked about any of it—we'd kissed until we were breathless with it, and then a particularly bright star had caught our attention, and she'd let me go and lay back down beside me. I'd been devastated, but I didn't know how to initiate it. I didn't know if she'd be okay with me initiating it. Maybe it had just been the heat of the moment, an emotional release in a shitty situation.

She'd dropped me off at the trailer in the gray light of early dawn, and I'd thought about leaning across the cab to kiss her goodbye, but in the end I'd just mumbled *Good night* and *Drive safe*, and I'd taken my things inside with me.

Cole's yearbook was full of scribbled messages and signatures from his classmates—some of them affectionate, some teasing, some hinting that half of my brother's graduating class had had a crush on him. I didn't spot any pictures of Jolene, but on the very last page, I found her signature.

Cole—your acceptance and friendship has meant the world to me, especially the past few weeks. I hope you get everything you want. You deserve to be happy. Love, Jolene Whitaker

I stared at it for a long, long time before something clicked.

"About a month before we graduated, I figured it out."

"Oh my God," I said aloud, re-reading it. *Acceptance* was a weird word for people who had known each other for years, wasn't it? Except she'd told him. She'd told my brother that she didn't—couldn't—love Johnny. She'd told him that she wanted to be with a woman instead.

And Cole, my precious brother, had just accepted her and kept being her friend. He hadn't told anyone, not even me. My eyes welled up with emotion, and I closed the yearbook reverently and tucked it back into the box. I settled the lid on top of it, then I climbed up into the daybed and nestled into the pillow.

"Cole," I whispered aloud, "I think... I think I might be like Jolene." The corner of my lips curled upward in an involuntary smile just saying her name aloud. "I think I might *like* Jolene. A lot."

And then I closed my eyes and drifted off to sleep, at peace with the knowledge that my brother would have accepted and loved me just the same even if he'd been alive to hear me say that.

* * *

When I finally woke up again late that evening, past dusk, distant stars peeking through the edges of the lavender sky, the house was dark. I found Johnny sitting in the kitchen, staring out the sliding glass door, a bottle of beer sweating on the table beside him. It was still mostly full.

"Where you been?" His voice was quiet, and I listened close, but I couldn't tell if he sounded angry.

"What? I was taking a nap in the junk room. Got tired cleaning stuff." Just a little white lie. Mostly true.

"That why there's two lunch bags and two thermoses on the kitchen counter?" He still hadn't looked at me, and I couldn't make myself take another step into the room, frozen on the thin metal threshold where the stained carpet turned to cracked linoleum. "That why there's fresh tire prints out in the yard?"

"Mandy Lynn came over to see how I was doing." First person who came to mind, Sunday school teacher's daughter. We'd gone to school together. Johnny and I had gone to her wedding when she married Jerry Lawson, the mechanic, two years after the accident. We'd had to pull the car to the side of the road halfway there so I could throw up, and we'd walked the rest of the way to the church. We'd gotten there about the time they'd come out, birdseed flying in a cloud around them, and I'd been secretly grateful I hadn't had to go inside.

"Funny thing." His voice cracked. I swallowed. "I called Jerry's shop when I got home from Meridian to see if maybe he had a transmission he could sell me for your car. Talked to Mandy Lynn. She said she hadn't seen you in ages, asked how you were."

"Maybe that was—"

His hand came down hard on the table. The bottle jumped, splashing little puddles onto the table. "Stop lyin' to me!"

I couldn't say anything else to him. The truth was out of the question.

He stood up so slowly I could almost hear his bones creak. He tore a paper towel from the roll, brought it back, and calmly cleaned up his spilled beer, all without looking at me. I felt like a bee trapped between the screen door and the glass pane, crawling aimlessly, knowing there was nowhere to fly but wanting to try it anyway. I felt like Jezebel and Judas all in one.

"Who is it?" He stood with his hands braced on the table, his shoulders slumped, his head hung low. He looked and sounded so, so tired. "Is it Kevin? I'd understand. He's rich. He'd be able to take care of you like you deserve, give you a nice wedding—"

"It's not Kevin. You know I don't care about money." That much was the truth, at least. I'd never given two minutes of thought to getting married. I didn't even know Kevin was single.

"Then who, Lil?" He turned his head to look at me. "Why?" His eyes were dark, hollow, and I felt so low I might as well have been on my belly in the dirt like the serpent in the garden when I realized he'd been crying. I'd done that to him.

I had to tell him the truth. I couldn't do this to him. To both of us.

"It's Jolene."

The silence stretched out thick and heavy while I waited for him to call down brimstone on my head.

He snorted.

"Jolene? Lil, I told you there ain't nothin' between us anymore. I barely even seen her since she's been back in town. Those gossipy old hens been telling you otherwise?"

"Not you and Jolene." I wet my lips and reached deep for the steel that all the books said I'd find in myself when I needed it the most. There was nothing there but a great dark hollow. My hands clenched on empty air. "Me. And Jolene."

I didn't even realize I was crying until a tear dripped off my chin and onto my arm. Johnny paused, then turned his body to face me, shoulders slumped like he hadn't been prepared for that to hit him straight on. Fair enough. I hadn't been, either.

"Wh..." He shook his head, and I waited for it to sink in. "*Jolene*? But...Lilly, you ain't... You ain't like that."

"Like what, Johnny?" My voice crumbled like one of my damn pie crusts. I guess it was too much to hope that he would accept my truth like Cole had accepted Jolene's.

He looked around like somebody might be hiding down our hallway to hear him, then hissed, "Like *that*. A... You know."

"No, I don't know!" My inhale was closer to a gasp, and I tried hard to stuff it down. "I don't know what! I don't know *nothin'*, Johnny. Nobody ever told me I could love a woman the way I've never loved a man. I didn't know, 'til she showed me."

He flinched at that, but I couldn't take it back. I couldn't tell him *except you*, because I was done lying. I loved Johnny in a way. He'd been good to me, and he was the only man I could even stand the thought of touching me, but I didn't ache for it, didn't yearn for him the way I couldn't stop thinking about Jolene's summer-green eyes and rain-soft lips.

"I'm sorry," I whispered, salt on my tongue. It was the best I could do. "I mean that."

He sank back into his chair, an empty, defeated shell of a man, and

I couldn't stand to be in the same room as the destruction I'd wrought. God, I wished I was brave enough to go with Jolene when she left. Maybe Aunt Pauline would take me back if I didn't tell her what I'd just told Johnny; or maybe the earth would crack itself open and swallow me up to be food for the worms.

A sharp noise out in the woods caught my attention, and then the barest flicker of movement, and I knew. I only saw a glimpse, a flash of blond hair, but I *knew.*

It was Cole.

I was out the back door before I could think twice about it. My feet never even touched the warped, peeling boards of the deck as I sailed down into the grass, stumbling and flailing as my body tried to freeze and fly at the same time.

"Lilly! Lilly Ann!"

Johnny's voice was a distant echo in another world, far away from me. The night air rattled in my lungs as I gulped it down. I didn't even feel the undergrowth pulling at me, tearing my clothes, my legs, my arms. I couldn't see the figure anymore, but I could see the leaves moving in his wake, and I followed desperately.

"Cole! Wait!"

The thick tangle gave way suddenly, and I pitched forward onto my hands between the twisted roots of the ancient oak tree that grew there. I struggled up to my feet—and there he was.

I froze, vision blurry as tears filled my eyes, but I refused to blink, refused to let him out of my sight for one moment. Standing in front of the oak tree was my brother, as he had been the last time I'd seen him alive. My parents had been driving him to Meridian, to the regional airport, where he would take the first of many flights to his deployment in Saudi Arabia. He'd been in the back seat of the car with me, bothering me while I tried to ignore him to read a book I would never finish. *Harper Lee, bloodstained mockingbird wings on the hospital table next to me when I woke...*

He smiled now like he had then—like he was being a nuisance on purpose and was delighted by it—and then he turned and vanished into the tree.

"No!" I screamed and lurched forward, slapping my palms against the oak tree like it could give my brother back. I knew it was hopeless —but then something glinted. There was a hole in the trunk, mostly grown together now, and there was something inside it. Something silver that caught the moonlight and winked at me.

One fingertip on my left hand could just brush the surface of cold metal, and I started trying to pull open the bark that had grown up around the hole, scraping at the scar. Then Johnny was there, grip like a vise on my wrists as he pulled me back, and I fought him every inch of the way.

"Lilly Ann, *stop*." He pressed my hands against his chest, and the streak of crimson against the dirty white fabric shocked me into still-ness. It was my blood; my hands were scraped raw, and the tree was no closer to giving up its secret.

"I saw something," I gasped. "Cole—wanted me to see it—"

Johnny's face twisted with pity. "Lilly..."

I yanked my hands out of his hold, furious and desperate. "I saw him!" I reached for the tree again, but Johnny blocked me, and I hit his chest with my reddened right hand. He barely flinched. "There's some-thing in there! Something in the tree. I have to know what he was trying to show me!"

"Okay." He held up his hands, a helpless gesture of appeasement, the shadows on his face making him look like he'd aged ten years in the past ten minutes. "Wait here. I'll get the hatchet."

I watched him go, stilled by the gravity that had settled over him. It sat on me too, heavy and thick in the night. A million heartbeats later he returned with a hefty metal file in one hand and his grandfather's hand-axe in the other. I flinched the first time the blade bit into the tree, chunks of freshly wounded wood falling to the ground.

Don't hurt it, I thought wildly, heart pounding in my throat. But it was just a tree; it didn't have feelings. Those were mine.

Once he had part of the growth chipped away, he switched to the file, grinding the edge down until it was smooth enough he wouldn't cut himself when he stuck his hand in. He came out with a dented metal lunchbox, rusted almost beyond recognition.

Almost, but not for me. I might not have *actually* been able to see Luke Skywalker past the pitted, flaky paint, but I knew he was there. I knew because I'd seen his face and his white robes on the schoolbus every morning until Cole had come home from ninth grade without that box one day and told my mother he'd lost it. She'd refused to buy him another one, and he'd taken his lunch to school in paper bags shoved into his backpack after that. I'd always assumed he'd been embarrassed to take it into high school with him and had ditched it somewhere.

But here it was, stuffed into the hollow heart of a tree in the very woods where he and Johnny had spent almost every weekend of their childhood—

A strangled sob cracked the silence, and I realized Johnny was gripping the lunchbox so hard his hands were shaking and his knuckles were turning white. The metal bowed and popped under his thumbs. "Damn it," he whispered. "Goddamn it, Cole…"

I reached for him before I could remember that he probably didn't want me anywhere near him anymore, before I remembered how fresh my betrayal was—and he didn't stop me. My hand settled awkwardly on his arm.

"Let's go inside," I said quietly. "Where it's light. And open it."

He shook his head hard and shoved the box at me. I fumbled it gracelessly, catching it against my chest, as I watched him stalk off. "You open it," he said as he crashed through the underbrush. "I don't want to see it."

About the time I was setting the box on the table, I saw the light come on in the lean-to out back and figured Johnny must taking out his feelings on one of his projects. God knew he had plenty of projects. Tonight, he had plenty of feelings too.

It took a flat edge screwdriver and some determination, but the lunchbox lid finally popped open. Inside, among some organic debris and a few odds and ends like a quarter and a couple of rocks, were

- a handful of photographs held together with a fragile rubber band,

- a cassette tape with *From Cole* written in faded blue ink on the label,
- and a folded piece of lined paper, the edge uneven with jagged little tabs from where it had been ripped out of a notebook.

I retrieved Johnny's Walkman and slid the cassette in carefully. I held my breath as I pressed Play; who knew if it still worked after all this time? But after a soft crackle, the warbly notes of The Smiths were in my ears.

Don't feel bad for me, I want you to know—

The photographs were next. The rubber band snapped almost as soon as I touched it, and the pictures slid into my hands, five of them. They were smaller than standard, like all the ones that had come from Cole's old plastic camera. Two were candid shots of Johnny, handsome and whimsical, dark hair pushed back with one impatient hand. In the first he was holding a cigarette close to his lips; in the other, he was looking at someone out of frame with such heat it should've scorched the paper. Jolene, probably. The next photograph was Cole, squinting into bright sunlight but laughing, his sandy blond hair slung wetly across his forehead, sunburned beneath his freckles, so happy it hurt to look at him. I stared at that picture for a long time before I moved on.

The next one, Cole had clearly held the camera out as far as he could and taken a picture of the two of them, their heads leaned together. It was crooked and off-center, too-close and a little out of focus, but it looked like it might have been around Christmas. Maybe the year Cole had gotten the camera; they both looked so incredibly young.

The very last one was Johnny, straight on, one hand mostly covering the camera lens. In the curve between the blur of his thumb and forefinger, though, he was smiling, his eyes so blue they took my breath away. God. How long had it been since I'd seen Johnny smile? Maybe as long as it had been since I'd seen Cole alive.

It took me a long time to lay the pictures aside, and only the siren call of the letter compelled me. Before I even opened it, though, I had a feeling I knew what I'd find. Through the eye of the camera, through the sound of music in the tattered headphones—the Cure, now, *nothing in the world that I ever wanted more*—I recognized in my brother the same heart-spinning, sideways longing I felt for Jolene... but for his best friend.

The paper was dated August 23, 1990, two days before the accident.

Johnny, it said, and I stopped. Reading on was an invasion of privacy...but I was afraid Johnny would destroy the letter if I gave it to him. Maybe I shouldn't read it, but seeing my brother's messy, scribbly handwriting felt like seeing him again, just for a second, and in the end, I couldn't look away.

This weekend I'm being shipped out. Thanks for promising to look out for Lilly Ann while I'm gone. She doesn't talk about it much but I know the popular girls give her a hard time at school, and she's shy.

I hope you'll meet me tomorrow night, like we talked about, but I'm writing this in case you don't. Or in case I chicken out and can't tell you. But I figure there's a good chance I'll die out in the desert, and if I do, I want you to know.

I stopped reading then, folding the letter and closing my eyes. No; the rest was between Johnny and Cole. I knew enough, now, to know that my brother and I were the same. I suddenly understood all of Jolene's held-back silences; she must have known, too. He must have told her, when she told him about herself. And if I hadn't loved her before, I knew I loved her then, for keeping my brother's secrets even after he was gone.

I heard the back door opening and closing as David Bowie sang wistfully about falling in love in a crumbling world—my heart squeezed thinking about that night in the theater, the four of us in an inescapable labyrinth of pieces we wouldn't understand about ourselves for years.

"Is it..." Johnny cleared his throat as he stepped up to the table, wiping his hands anxiously on a tattered red hand towel that he kept out in his shed. When he spoke again, his voice sounded equally threadbare. "There were things...in it? From Cole?"

I turned, lowering the headphones and gently stopping the cassette tape. "Yes," I said quietly. "I think they're all for you."

Johnny's face screwed up tight, and he dragged one palm over his eyes and then his mouth. What an awful gauntlet the Guthrie siblings had put this poor man through today.

"I'll rewind the tape for you," I offered quietly. "And fix you a glass of tea."

He nodded, swallowing so hard I heard the click in his throat. "Thanks."

He washed his hands in the bathroom while I set the tea down on a folded paper towel, well out of the way of the delicate photographs and letter. The creak of the wooden chair when he sank into it reached all the way through the center of me, and I touched his shoulder gently before I left him in the kitchen with my brother's ghost.

I had a phone call to make before the line was cut off forever.

Fourteen

The truck didn't have to be hotwired, and my suitcase fit behind the seat. The two remaining boxes of my family's keepsakes were tied down under a tarp in the truck bed, the paltry sum of my earthly possessions.

I clutched Cole's dented lunchbox in my lap. Johnny had kept the photos, the letter, and the cassette tape, but he'd put the last of my pie money, Cole's ring, and my fortune cards in the box and handed it to me. I still hadn't managed to swallow the lump in my throat that had lodged there when he'd hugged me—cautious, for so many reasons, but genuine—and said, *"You tell him it wasn't because I didn't try."*

I still didn't know if he'd meant keeping his promise to look out for me, or returning my brother's impossible feelings. Maybe both. Maybe something else altogether.

"I'll tell him," I'd promised.

Jolene turned her cassette tape over to Side B in the player but turned the volume down, watching me. "You ready?"

We didn't know where we were going. Neither of us had anyone beyond the borders of Gideon to offer guidance or shelter. All we had was a road map, Jolene's inheritance from Miss Agnes, and about fifty dollars in pie money. Once we passed Meridian, there was a whole wide world out there waiting just for us.

I thought again, not for the first time, about flipping over a card or two, just to see if they offered any hints—a cardinal direction, toward water or away from it, into the mountains or to the sea—but in the end, I decided that I wanted to turn that page for myself without peeking ahead. I wanted the world to surprise me.

And for the first time in more than five years, I wasn't lying when I said, "I'm ready."

The End

Bonus Story

"Secrets in the Walls"
a gift for a stranger

* * *

Summers in Chickasaw have always been hot. Worse, they're humid. The air hangs sodden and still, like a wet woolen blanket weighing you down. Right about June, it gets so that you can't breathe, children and dogs sprawled out on the porch, longing for a breeze. When I was a kid, we didn't have air conditioning, not really. Lazy ceiling fans pushed the air around but didn't cool it, and in the afternoons, my sisters fought over who got to sit in front of Mother's metal fan that rattled and hummed in a futile war against the heat.

Daddy worked long hours to keep us fed. Well, he did when he had a job. Every six months or so, he had to find a new one, and the more jobs he lost, the fewer he could find, and the further he retreated into his bottles.

Mother stayed busy with the Ladies' Auxiliary at the church, gathering clothes people had outgrown and donating them. We'd had a few "Auxiliary clothes" ourselves. They always fit just a little irregular, but

Mother would take them up with her sewing machine and we'd wear them until we outgrew them or wore holes in them.

I helped her sometimes, and as many times as she said "Idle hands are the devil's playground," nobody had ever thought to warn me that busy hands weren't always safe. I never thought I was a wicked child, but I must have been, because only the wicked could steal from charity.

At first I didn't take much—a string of plastic pearls, scuffed so that they wouldn't be of use to anyone. They might have even been thrown away, but I tucked them into my pocket before anyone could. After that it was a pair of clip-on earrings, the emeralds so obviously made of paste that the green paint was chipping off. But then it got worse, and I had to find somewhere to hide it. I didn't have anywhere at home that I could keep a dress, a silk-flowered Easter hat, and a pair of shoes with pretty little bows on them.

I felt bad for stealing them, but I told myself it wasn't like we didn't sometimes get outfits from the Auxiliary, and someone was going to be getting them, anyway. The only reason I took them without asking was because Mary Alice would have gotten them instead. They fit her better than they did me, and she was the oldest so she always got the nicer things.

The stealing wasn't my real sin. Maybe my real sin was wanting to keep for myself what should have been my sister's.

It didn't take me long at all to work out where to keep my contraband. The old gray house at the end of our street had been abandoned since the Great Depression, and twenty years is a long time for a house to be empty. It was huge, with boarded up windows that stared like empty eyes and walls that slumped to one side like a tired old woman at the end of a long day's work. Spanish moss hung from the spreading water oaks around it like torn veils. A swamp in the back was home to bullfrogs and cicadas that sang all summer long, making a racket so loud you couldn't hear yourself think over the sound.

Everybody was scared to go near the place. Grown-ups said it was "structurally unsound." Kids said it was haunted. My little sister Daisy said she thought it was a robber's hide-out. I thought it looked lonely and like the perfect keeper for my secret.

One afternoon in mid-July, while Mary Alice and Daisy were sharing an uneasy truce in front of the fan, Mother was patching clothes with the Auxiliary Ladies, and Daddy was helping the preacher do some repairs on the roof of the church—it wasn't a real job, but it kept him out of the bottle, and Reverend Mason wanted to do what he could to help—I sneaked into the old gray house and into the room that held my treasure.

I closed the door behind me, took off my clothes, dropped them in the corner, and shimmied into that dress. It was a little loose in the front—my chest was much flatter than my sister's—but the skirt flared out just perfectly above the bow-tied shoes, and the brim of the hat dipped down gracefully over one of my eyes. I wished my hair was longer, maybe in pretty ringlets like Mary Alice's, so I could look just like a storybook princess. I put on the plastic pearls and the chipped clip-on earrings, and I twirled.

Mother didn't approve of twirling, said it wasn't ladylike. She'd rapped Mary Alice's fingers for it once, told her to stop showing her unmentionables to all the boys. But there was no one to see me in the old gray house, so I twirled until I was dizzy and sick.

When I stopped, too breathless for the giggle hanging in my chest like a prism in the sun, shooting rainbows of happiness all through me, I imagined that I was a princess trapped in a tower. The witch who'd put me here had cut off all my hair so I couldn't lower it for a prince to climb up the tower, but he would come anyway, his boots dusty from riding miles and miles to find me. He would kill the witch and run up the stairs. I would hear his footsteps and know—

The stairs creaked.

I held my breath, my heart beating against my chest like a moth in a glass jar. I waited, but there was nothing—nothing but the cicadas buzzing outside and the thumping in my ears. I let my breath out slowly, still listening.

My hands shook as I smoothed down the skirt of my dress, as I regarded the walls of the lonely house, my old friend. Had someone seen? Was someone watching? Ice in my stomach made me go cold all over, shivering in the summer heat.

There was nowhere to go. I wanted to put my own clothes back on, not my stolen princess dress, but I was afraid to undress. What if someone could see me?

But there were no more sounds, and eventually I began to relax. It was just an old house, settling in the heat. There were no peepers, no robbers hiding out, no ghosts, just me and my silly imagin—

—the door to my secret room opened, swung slowly inward on a whisper. My breath caught in my throat, my vision went bright around the edges, and as I watched, a dusty brown shoe appeared.

My scream caught in my throat, strangled and nearly soundless, but that brown shoe took a quick step back and the owner gave a quick shout of surprise. The door swung the rest of the way open, and Billy Ray Mason, the preacher's son, stared at me like a scared rabbit, cowering against the opposite wall.

I let out the rest of my breath in a shaky rush, but a new fear settled in my stomach. The dress—the hat—the shoes—What would he think? His daddy was the preacher. Surely—

"You scared the livin' daylights outta me!" He bent over at the middle, gasping for air, and I slid down to sit on the floor, the skirt of my dress pooling around me like a puddle of sin. "What on earth are you doin' up here?"

I couldn't answer, too full of trembling and fighting back tears. He would tell his daddy, and then my daddy would get angry, and he'd start drinking again, and—

"Hey, are you crying?"

"No." I scraped my knuckles over my face, shoving away the tears. "S'just sweat."

"I didn't mean to scare you." He hovered over me, standing stiff and awkward. "I... Uh, that sure is a pretty dress. Where'd you get it?"

My eyes started leaking again and I ducked my head farther. Guilt and shame pounded in my chest and I muttered, "I stole it."

"Oh." He sat down in front of me, crossed his legs, and offered me the handkerchief out of his pocket. It was dirty, and I stared at it. He looked embarrassed but didn't take it back, and I gingerly took it from him.

"From the Ladies' Auxiliary." The confession spilled out of me so fast I couldn't even hold it in. "I took the pearls first, then the earrings —they're not real pearls, and the earrings are just clip-ons, see?—but then the hat was so pretty—and the dress was perfect for being a princess, and—" I snapped my mouth shut so fast I nearly bit my tongue.

"So you come up here to be a princess?" He looked around the room, no doubt seeing how I'd swept the floor with an old straw broom, my clothes in the corner, the old broken coat rack I used to hang the dress when I wasn't there.

He didn't seem angry, didn't seem scandalized to be sitting with a sinner. Maybe he wouldn't tell his daddy after all. Maybe I could tell him more.

"Princess Caroline." I couldn't believe I'd said it out loud, and I ducked my head. I was too old to be playing childish games, putting on dresses and twirling—

"It suits you." His grin was big and wide in his face. "You make a great princess." He didn't look like he was making fun of me, and something fluttered in my belly, something bright and erratic, like fire-flies. He laughed, and the fluttering started to turn sick before he took my hand. "For a second, when I heard you, I really thought the house was haunted! I 'bout wet my pants."

I laughed, surprised, and tried not to look at where his hand was gripping mine. Maybe if I didn't look, he wouldn't notice, and he wouldn't stop touching me.

"What are you doing up here, anyway?"

He shrugged, looking away for a moment. "Lost a game of ring taw, didn't want to give up my shooter. Paul and Harry said they'd let me keep *all* my marbles, not just the shooter, if I came in here and stayed for five minutes."

I jumped, letting go of his hand to grab my hat and pull it off, scared to death. If Paul and Harry saw me, they'd for *sure* tattle, and—

"They ain't close." Billy Ray must've read my mind. He put his hand on my arm, stilling me. "They was too scared."

I relaxed, but only a little. "I just don't..."

"It's okay. I won't tell." He looked at me kind of funny, and I wanted to put the hat back on, to hide behind its wide brim, but that would just be silly. He shifted on the floor, stretching out one leg to the side. I stared at the patch on the knee of his pants to keep from seeing his face. The stitching was neat and even, but even the patch was starting to get worn through. Maybe he wore Auxiliary clothes too. I bet his momma—

—The quick press of his lips against mine was wet and startling and over before I knew what was happening. I gasped, staring at him wide-eyed, and he looked as scared as I'd ever seen anyone look, like he thought I might deck him for it.

"Sorry," he mumbled. "That was stupid. I just thought—princesses get kissed, right?" He looked up at me, and all the fireflies in my stomach glowed bright and frenzied, zooming around like they were trying to get out.

"Billy Ray! It's been five minutes! You still alive?"

The voice outside made me duck down as if they could see through the boarded-up windows on the second story, as if they could see my lips still burning from that kiss.

Billy Ray gave me a sad smile. "I'd better go down before they get brave enough to come check on me. Or worse, go find my daddy and tell him where I am." He got up and dusted his pants off, shouting down to Paul and Harry, "I'm comin'! Keep your britches on!"

He looked down at me and hesitated. "If you want... I'll wait for you downstairs and walk you home. I'll yell up when Paul and Harry are gone."

I didn't want, not really, but I couldn't say no without being rude, and he'd been so nice. He hadn't been mean about the dress, and he wasn't going to tattle on me.

"All right."

He smiled and ran downstairs, his boots so loud on the creaking steps, so different from when he'd first come creeping in. As soon as he was out of the room, I scrambled out of the dress and back into my clothes. I looked for a place to hide the dress and hat just in case Paul and Harry decided to be brave, but there wasn't anywhere, so I just hung it back on the hat rack and hoped they wouldn't think it had anything to do with me.

It seemed like forever before Billy Ray called up to me, and I crept down the stairs, still half-expecting to find myself facing a firing squad when I left the house. It wasn't possible for Billy Ray to just not tell anyone, was it? Would he really keep my secret?

But he was alone, no one with him to ask why I'd been in the old house. He didn't say anything else about it as we walked to my house either, instead telling me all about how he'd told Paul and Harry the house was haunted.

"I told them I heard a woman screaming when I got to the second floor, and footsteps on the stairs." He grinned at me, mischief in his eyes. "You shoulda seen their faces! They were so scared!" He puffed up his chest like a rooster, and I tried not to laugh. "And the best part is I didn't even lie to 'em!"

I faltered a little at that. Of course Billy Ray wouldn't lie. What if he—

The sight of my parents standing on the front porch of our house, talking to Billy Ray's parents, stopped my train of thought in a wreck of nerves.

"There you two are!" My mother crossed her arms, but she was smiling. "We've been wondering where you were. We're about to have lunch, so run wash up real fast!"

I darted a quick look at Daddy as I ran past, happy when I could tell he looked sober. He seemed more relaxed, too, like working had made him feel good. Maybe he'd even stay out of the bottle tonight.

Billy Ray and I jockeyed for the sink in the bathroom, laughing and splashing water on each other, and just looking at him made me smile. I remembered in the old house, the way he'd touched my hand, the way he'd kissed me, and...

"Boys, hurry up in there! Lunch is ready!"

My breath caught in my throat, and I looked at Billy Ray in the mirror. For a while, I had forgotten. I had just been Caroline, maybe a princess, definitely a girl. Maybe Billy Ray had forgotten, too. Maybe now—

Billy Ray made a mock bow and gestured to the door. "After you, my lady," he said, and all the fireflies inside me must have lit up all at the same time, because I *glowed*.

ACKNOWLEDGMENTS

This story has been a passion project of mine for over four years at the time of publication, and I owe so much to the people who supported it and me along the way.

Courtney, who not only put up with endless "how does this sound?" questions, but also gave Cole his name and introduced me to Tay, whose beautiful cover art brought the characters to life.

Skye Kilaen, who as always is such a support that I'm not sure how or if this book would exist without her. It's impossible to detail all the ways in which she enabled this project.

Kelsey Allagood, Becca Podos, and K.A. Mitchell for encouraging my foray into this style of prose with their invaluable feedback.

And finally, the baristas at my local coffee shop for all the iced coffees and lavender matchas, and to my family for their time, understanding, and encouragement.

Thank you all.

About the Author

Jules Kelley writes character-central fiction from her home in lovely Central Florida. The details and settings may vary, but she always loves weird characters most—misfits, monsters, and messy humans just trying their best—and writes to share them with the world so you can love them too.

Please consider leaving a review, and thank you for reading!

Find more works from Jules on her website:
https://juleskelleybooks.com

Follow her on Tumblr:
https://www.tumblr.com/blog/juleskelleybooks

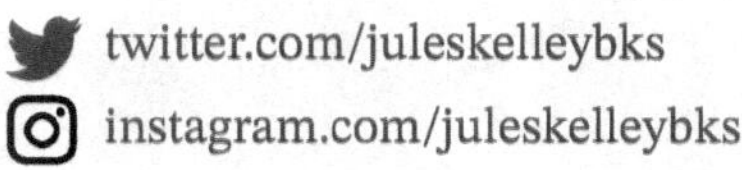

twitter.com/juleskelleybks
instagram.com/juleskelleybks